The Phantom Spy

Also by Max Brand

The Phantom Spy

MAX BRAND

A Novel of Adventure

Dodd, Mead & Company · New York

ISBN: 0-396-06745-X
Library of Congress Catalog Card Number: 72-7753
Printed in the United States of America
by Vail-Ballou Press, Inc., Binghamton, N. Y.

The Phantom Spy

CHAPTER ONE

ON THE first floor there was a view of the dirty little Rue Morat as far as the English chemist's, and on that floor lived the concierge and his wife, who beat him whenever she drank absinthe and read Victor Hugo. The owner of the building lived there also, partly because nobody else would use the rooms and partly because of the wife of the concierge. On three floors above the view of the Rue Morat extended as far as the trees of the square. But the fifth floor overlooked the world of Paris roofs and even saw the sky.

Through that upper world stray cats wandered among dormer windows, chimney pots, washings, broken tiles, but inside the fifth floor windows lived Persian rugs in a great studio room, paintings that were not of the modern school, tall mirrors which looked at them, an Henri Quatre bed that was too beautiful to be quite decent, and finally, Lady Cecil, daughter of an earl who was such a patriot that he rarely saw Paris even when Cecil was there.

On this evening, Lady Cecil had just been helped into a cloak with a chinchilla collar which she liked because it cost so much and because chinchilla was so out of fashion. The telephone rang and Cecil Margaret Agnes Kathryn De

Waters picked up the receiver. "Yes?" she said.

Over the telephone breathed the strains of an accordion so well played that it sounded like an organ in the distance, with wood-winds supporting.

And a rich voice sang:

> *Was macht er in den schwarzen Wald,*
> *Arme Willie, arme Willie?*
> *Was macht er in den . . .*

"Willie Gloster!" cried Cecil. "Oh, Willie, I didn't know you were in town. What are you doing?"

"I'm going to be your darling this evening," said Gloster.

"I mean, will you join us—"

"I can't join us, because I despise him," said Gloster.

"You don't even know him," said Cecil. "He's a charming Belgian—"

"There aren't any charming Belgians. You know that," said Gloster.

"He's the exception," said the girl.

"He's a *sans nous,*" said Gloster.

"No, he's too young for that."

"The whole damned world is too young for anything. *You're* too young," declared Gloster.

"Willie, he's really nice and we'd love to have you. I'm not too young either."

"Too young for what?" asked Gloster.

"I won't let you trip me up," she told him.

"You don't seem to get the point," said Gloster. "The point is that this evening Cecil is going to have Willie all to himself—*herself,* I mean to say. Why do you wear a man's name, Margaret Agnes Kathryn? It makes me feel a little odd."

"A family idiosyncrasy, Willie," she answered. "And

2

aren't you just a little drunk, darling?"

"Only a little, and the rest is for you," said Gloster. "Just phone the Belgian that it's all over. Tell him I'm in town and he'll understand, if he understands anything. I'll be right over."

"I suppose I'll meet you some place, then," said Cecil.

"Of course you will," he told her. "You'll meet me in your place!"

"I can't feed you, Willie. I've let the cook go."

"That's all right," he decided. "You're a beautiful cook."

"I can hardly cook at all," she said.

"You're a beautiful cook," he said. "I'll be right over."

"Willie!" she cried.

But the telephone went dead in her ear.

She hung up and looked at the maid. A comforting quality of French servants is that always they have thought the worst of you almost from the beginning.

"Estelle," she said, "you may go, rather quickly, but first telephone to Monsieur Brisson and say that I'm suddenly ill, so sorry about tonight, but simply unable to go out."

Lady Cecil, while this message was being sent, got slowly and thoughtfully out of her cloak, and as the maid disappeared for the night the telephone rang again. Lady Cecil hesitated about answering, in case it might be Brisson making a last appeal; but the telephone was insistent, and at last she picked it up.

London calling Lady Cecil. Mr. R. would speak with her. . . .

She caught her breath. She never had seen the mainspring of the English secret service. It was said that he chose to dress like a relic of the Gladstone era; that he had soft manners, gentle and soothing; but ah, the stories she had heard about him since she had offered herself, at her own expense, to the silent service of England.

3

His voice came now over the wire. She knew by its quality that people in the room where he was would hardly be able to make out his words, and yet they came through, quietly and distinctly, to her ear. At all times Mr. R. maintained the intense calm of a gambler who has put his entire fortune on a single card and will not betray the least emotion. A force like accumulating static electricity began to store up in her as she listened.

"We've been sorry to have you gone so long," said Mr. R. "We've missed you a great deal but now we find it lucky that you're in Paris; because what do you think—Maggie's picture is gone . . . stolen . . . and poor Papa Jacques knows nothing about it. Isn't that a pity?"

Maggie—the Maginot Line. Her picture—the maps of the great system of fortifications along the Eastern frontier—Papa Jacques—the French people. Lady Cecil made these translations with a dizzy brain, for no one had spoken to her before about such important matters as the Maginot Line. She felt herself caught up to a height of danger and of glory even before she heard the rest of what that quiet voice in her ear had to say:

"The picture is now," went on Mr. R., "in the hands of a big, blond young man with a bursting laugh and pale blue eyes. He uses the name of Axel Hendriksen and he is stopping for the evening at the only hotel in the little town of Grossenhain, near Freiberg in the Black Forest. He will be there probably for several hours because he is celebrating. Then he will start on. He is using a long-nosed, powerful gray Mercedes and he drives fast. His road will take him toward Berchtesgaden . . . and I thought that if you were able to overtake him and explain to him what a bad thing it is to steal Maggie's picture, perhaps he would give it back to your safekeeping. I know you have some friends in Paris who would be glad to help you, and you're such a grown-up

4

girl that I thought I would leave the whole matter in your hands. . . ."

When the soft voice no longer sounded and the huge vision of London had withdrawn at the click of the receiver, her first impulse was to rush at once to the St. Cloud airfield and hire a plane but she realized that she could do little by herself. She knew what Mr. R. meant by her friends in Paris. To help herself visualize them, she wrote down their names in a rapid list.

Their voices and faces flowed in upon her, and suddenly it seemed to Lady Cecil that the great British Empire was a pitiful thing indeed if it could hire only such dolts for its secret service. One of them was a fighting man; one had a fine, persuasive tongue; one had a touch of talent for deciphering code—the rest were nothing. She had to make haste but it was better not to go at all than to start with the wrong equipment.

A ring at the door tumbled her out of her lofty problem to the thought of William Gloster. He was an unusual fellow who had pyramided his fortune to a heap of millions by the time he was twenty-five and who had spent the years since the market crashed playing around the world and storing in his heart an enormous, almost drunken good humor. She wanted no Gloster now. She wanted a sober brain, hard, polished, and edged.

Outside the door she heard the accordion jittering through a Hungarian dance; when she opened up, the music and Gloster walked in upon her.

The accordion squawked as he collapsed it and dropped it into his pocket, for it was a miniature no bigger than a toy.

"Stand back, De Waters, and let me look at you," said Gloster. "I'm going to waste thirty seconds just looking at you. Can you take it?"

She had so much on her mind that when she looked at him he seemed much younger and taller than she remembered; his husky build ordinarily made him appear no more than average height. There was nothing soft and pudgy or merely fat about his solidity; his bulk was all strength as only one man's in a million is. He had a good-humored, grinning face, weather-darkened, with a good deal of red worked into the tan. He had heavy features and a great, retreating forehead covered with intellectual bumps like a pair of fists.

She saw her own image in a side mirror. Her dress was the color of a rose with so much yellow that the sun seemed to be shining on it.

"Don't pretend to be dazzled, Willie," she said.

"I thought I'd only imagined it, but it's truer than ever. Have you grown lovelier, Cecil, while I was away? Have you done that to me?"

"I've grown thinner," said Cecil.

He looked at her again. "Well, here you are, and here I am, and everything," said Gloster. "Kiss me, De Waters, will you?" She stepped inside his arms, but hesitated. "What's the delay?" he asked.

"I'm just looking you over."

"It isn't caution you need. It's time. How old are you, De Waters? Eighteen now?"

"I was eighteen the year you pulled me out of the crevasse, you idiot," said Lady Cecil.

"That was only yesterday. My God, De Waters, you're a beautiful damned thing. Will you marry me?"

"Presently," she said. "By the way, time has done plenty to you. It's given you enough—distance."

"De Waters, do you love me?"

"Why, of course."

"I mean, as only a good woman can love?"

"Willie, I don't like this," she said. "Go on and kiss

me, if you want to. But then stop, will you?"

"I don't want to kiss you," said Gloster. "I want to marry you. Do you love me, De Waters, or shall I go home?"

"I love you," said Lady Cecil. "What have you got in that briefcase?"

"I've got some presents for you," he said.

"What are they, darling?"

"Dog licenses," he said.

He opened the bag and poured out a lot of little metal tags. "I visited the pound and got licenses for all the dogs in it. They're all made out in your name. They'll be called for by De Waters tomorrow. . . . I'll have a drink, now. Brandy and soda. Old brandy. I'll go with you to fetch it. Don't try to shuffle out of my sight. . . . There's something else in this briefcase. You look at it while I make the drink."

They were in the white of the pantry as he poured his drink from a fat-bellied bottle and mixed in a dash of soda. She took the briefcase from under his arm and drew out a flat parcel. She was undoing it as they walked back from the pantry over the Persian rugs of the living room. At last she uncovered a painting of a square-faced man whose folded hands rested on the lower edge of the picture and whose eyes looked at eternity with a truly Germanic calm.

"What is it?" cried Lady Cecil.

"You'd better find out, because it's yours," said Gloster.

"It's not a Memling!" she gasped. "It's not really a Memling. Willie, you darling!"

"Back up," said Gloster. "It's a wedding present. I'm only leaving it with you in trust."

"I could almost marry you now!"

"What a good liar God made when he made you," said Gloster. "There's something eternal about you, De Waters,

7

something forever added to the spirit of modern man. Give me another drink."

"You have the bottle there . . . But *please,* Willie!"

"Alcohol is a necessity," said Gloster. "It is the necessary solvent that frees us from the past and the future and fixes us in the present as on a moving ship. Note that moving of the present moment, for motion is pure delight when no destination is in mind. Merely to travel—nowhere—is like . . . being in love with De Waters."

"Will you stop using that damned name and listen to me?" she begged. "You only can stay five more minutes."

"I laugh in your face, Margaret Agnes Kathryn."

"Because I'm in trouble that you can't help me out of. And I have to be alone and think my way out."

"I can't help you? Who could?"

"Hardly anybody . . . yes, somebody like that I suppose."

She pointed to a copy of the journal *La Liberté* which lay on the table. The great headline which stalked across the front page announced:

M. JACQUELIN REVEALED

"Monsieur Jacquelin?" said Gloster, "I've read that. Pure rot. I know Cailland, too. Not a bad fellow, but that article of his is rot, really."

"It's not rot," she declared. "Everybody knows that Jules Cailland is the only man Jacquelin ever worked with, and now Cailland is telling the truth about everything. The world is going to learn the story of the greatest international spy that ever lived! Think of it, Willie."

"Tripe," said Gloster. "The whole thing's drivel. Cailland doesn't even describe his Jacquelin."

"He does! He does!" cried the girl. "A big, powerful man

with a hint of the Oriental in his face. Isn't that a description? And he gives every detail of that tremendous thing in Georgia. . . . Isn't that telling?"

"Balderdash," said Gloster. "A cooked-up yarn with a Georgian princess in it."

"Oh, Willie, there are things that you just don't know about. A whole world of them! Everything that Cailland says is true. He promises eventually to publish the name Jacquelin lives under now, and even his photograph. . . . Poor Jacquelin! That's his death sentence, of course!"

"Why death sentence?"

"Because when he's identified how many nations will want to snatch him and third-degree him till he tells what he knows about their enemies? Even the countries he's worked for won't dare to let him live! The moment his picture appears in the paper, he's dead. Don't you see that—how horrible it is?"

"Why," said Gloster, "if this Jacquelin is half the man the story makes him out, doesn't he walk up to Jules Cailland and cut his throat to stop the stories?"

"Even Jacquelin can't do that," she answered. "Cailland's living in the offices of *La Liberté*. They've surrounded him with armed guards. No one can get in to speak with him except the editor of the paper. The whole world is going wild with his story on Monsieur Jacquelin. Didn't you read the late editions? A dozen countries have made representations to the French government, they say. The press of the whole world is reprinting the story on its front page."

"Know something, Cecil? You're so lovely that you almost seem to be making good sense. But let me tell you . . . all this stuff is perfect rot. . . . This Jacquelin is a dressed-up ghost. . . . Nobody even knows his real name. . . . They say he's not Jacquelin at all, but a German called Jocklein, or an Italian called d'Aquilino, or a Dutchman,

Jaakleen; but if he exists at all he's probably an ex-pig-raiser from Missouri called Jacklin."

Cecil wasn't listening. She was thinking. "Willie Gloster," she said suddenly, "would you help me?"

"I'd rather punch Monsieur Jacquelin on his Oriental nose; but of course I'll help you. Bring on the code and I'll break it to pieces."

"It isn't a code. It's something frightfully more important."

"Come, come," said Gloster. "In these spy yarns the breaking of a code is always the *pièce de résistance.*"

"Willie, did you fly to Paris in your own plane?"

"I did. I'll take you up tomorrow and show you how small France is. But wait a minute, my dear. What the devil do you mean by all this trouble that only a Jacquelin can help you out of? What sort of trouble is it? Hold on—have you let yourself into this damned eavesdropping, gum-shoeing business?"

"Willie, can I trust you? Kiss me, and tell me I can trust you, absolutely."

Gloster put his thick fingers under her chin and tilted her head a little. After a moment he said, "We'll save that for a while. This begins to sound like business to me."

Chapter Two

IN THE hotel at Grossenhain most of the people were drinking beer and listening to the violin and piano at the back
of the building, but Axel Hendriksen walked up and down
along the veranda at the front of the house where only a
faint throbbing of rhythm and thin drone of strings got to
his ear.

On the veranda there was music of another sort, for a
hefty American sat in a corner playing on an absurd little
accordion with his big hands, keeping the sound very small
so that it was like a confidential voice speaking to the girl
beside him. It was the girl who kept Hendriksen near. She
had appeared at the tavern so late that evening, with the
American, that Hendriksen had not had many opportunities
of talking with her; but even so, he knew that she was
pleasantly aware of him.

To judge by her awkward clothes, the American must
have picked her up in some neighboring village, and it was
delightful to watch her efforts to make eye and hand tell
him what her German tongue could not. At any rate, she
was a prize. If she had known how to wear her hair and
her hat, what a beauty she might have been!

11

So Hendriksen lingered near her. He was apparently engrossed in the mountains that jump up around Grossenhain, bristling with a dark beard of pines below and offering above, for the strong legs of German walkers, sharp chins and bald heads of rock, now sleeked over by the moonlight. But Hendriksen's eye was chiefly on the open doors of the garage inside of which two mechanics were struggling with the engine of his Mercedes. They had strong electric lights hitched on long cables. Sometimes their shadows made a gigantic step along the white of the wall but usually they were bent in labor and thought.

Hendriksen tried not to be impatient because of the delay. They had assured him that it would not be long before they found the trouble—something wrong with the electric current, or the timing. In France he might have felt despair, but the Germans are keen, patient mechanics, lacking something of Yankee intuition in dealing with machinery, but safe and sure in the long run. It could not be anything important because the car had been running perfectly when he reached Grossenhain, but any delay was important: in that car was something that meant a prize to Hendriksen. Two-hundred-thousand dollars in hard cash of which his share was sixty-thousand. Sixty-thousand dollars in gold, payable in any part of the world he chose to name; and good will along with the payment. The secret good will of a great nation!

Hendriksen swallowed the joy that came up like a song in his throat. Sixty-thousand out at five percent. That meant at least partial financial security for his entire future. But there was more and more money to be made in the great jungle of warring nations with adventure blowing like a sweet, pure wind in the face.

The hefty American was playing a jazz tune on the accordion, a silly new thing called "Anyhow," and translating it freely into German for the benefit of the girl. He knew how to sing. His voice was deep, the resonance of it was just a trifle nasal, and the words of his German translations, Hendriksen now discovered, were not even faintly related to the real words of the song. For the American sang, softly:

> Is it the wind that has ruffled your hair?
> Is it the night wind
> That has blown the stars into your eyes?
> Or is it love that has made you mysterious?

Hendriksen, walking with a soft step, listening, saw the improvised words of the song reflected on the face of the girl. He smiled a little as he turned to walk back along the veranda.

"Ah, he laughs!" said the girl. "That Norwegian gentleman knows English and he laughs, and you have made up all those words!"

"No," said the chunky man. "I only spoke the words that I found."

"Where did you find them?" asked the girl.

"Here. In this corner of the veranda. On the edge of the moonlight. Between the music and the mountains. . . ."

As Hendriksen turned again toward them, he saw the girl laughing happily. She shook her finger at Hendriksen as though to deny that she had believed a word of the translation. The chunky fellow smiled up at the Norwegian.

"You shouldn't laugh," he said. "Not when I'm doing my best."

Hendriksen, pausing, could not help laughing again. "I'm sorry," he said. "But I've heard 'Anyhow' sung rather differently."

The other stood up. He was inches shorter than the rangy Hendriksen. "My name's Gloster," he said. "Out

13

Wyoming way, if you know America."

Hendriksen shook hands and introduced himself.

"Auf Wiedersehen!" said the girl, slipping away.

"Ah—but wait!" called Gloster, stretching a hand after her.

"No. You're through with me," she answered, and disappeared through the doorway.

"Funny, aren't they?" asked Gloster.

"Germans?" said Hendriksen.

"Girls."

"Go on after her," suggested Hendriksen. "She wants you to."

"No," sighed Gloster. "She doesn't, really. I just fill in between the big shots. I keep the stage warm for them. That's all. She's looking for some real interest now. Hell, isn't it?"

He seemed partly in earnest as he laughed. Even while he talked, he was working the accordion softly, producing barely audible chords and stray tags of musical phrases. The thumb that pushed the bellows in and out also touched the stops and the four fingers employed themselves instinctively on the keys.

"You having trouble with your car?" Gloster asked, with that helpful friendliness which is peculiar to the American race.

"The wiring, something like that," said Hendriksen.

"Why, I ought to take a look at it," said Gloster. "Electricity's my middle name."

"Will you give it a look, then?" asked Hendriksen eagerly, offering to lead the way.

Gloster went along with him.

In the garage the American moved idly around the Mercedes. Now and then a phrase of music came whispering from the little miniature accordion. Sometimes he sat on his heels and stared. The German mechanics looked at him with disgust and turned muttering to their work.

"You can't make it out?" asked Hendriksen, a trifle annoyed by this casual attitude.

"The way I look at it," said Gloster, "the best thing usually is to get a slant first and see the drift of things; then. . . ."

He leaned suddenly over the open engine, pulled at something, and stepped back. "Try the starter," he suggested.

Hendriksen, shrugging his shoulders, reached over the instrument board and touched the starter; the engine roared an instant answer and the two mechanics shouted with astonishment. They gaped at Gloster, who was dusting his fingers and grinning.

"What in the world did you do?" asked Hendriksen.

"You know where the wires go up beside the carburetor like this?" asked Gloster, twisting his fingers into a design. "You take—"

"I don't know anything about the insides of a car," said Hendriksen. "But I'm grateful."

"Why, that's all right," said Gloster. "Glad to lend a hand. It'll probably stay all right for a while. You can get it fixed when you hit a big town."

"You mean it's apt to go wrong on me again tonight?" demanded Hendriksen.

"How far you going?"

"Only fifty miles or so."

"Well, I don't know," said Gloster, putting his big head on one side and then shaking it. "Maybe it'll be all right. I guess it'll be all right."

A car started up in front of the hotel and spun along the road. Hendriksen followed it with yearning eyes, he longed so much to be traveling in the same direction. A beam of light from the porch of the tavern, striking through the windows of the automobile, showed him the faintest glimpse of a woman's face in front, and by the beauty of the outline he recognized the girl who had been with Gloster.

It seemed a little strange that she should be starting off alone, and slightly stranger still that a person in such clothes should be the owner of an automobile, no matter how small. But he had something else to occupy his mind, and he looked earnestly at Gloster. His own motor, apparently, was apt to break down at any moment. Therefore he needed exactly the brains that this clever Yankee possessed; but to take a stranger into the car with him would be for Hendriksen a move of the greatest danger.

Therefore he made an effort to estimate the American with a clear and critical eye; yet he could not penetrate an inch beneath the surface of bursting good nature and vigorous buoyancy that Gloster presented to the casual glance. The man might be almost anything behind that screen, but Hendriksen decided to take the risk.

"Look here," he said, "will you go along and fix the damned thing if it pops out of order again?"

"Ah, I'm sorry," said Gloster. "I'm terribly sorry, but . . . ."

"It's worth a lot to me," said Hendriksen. "I'd pay anything to get away from here tonight. A hundred would be cheap. It really would. And I'd send you back again." He had been studying Gloster's old, rather shoddy clothes.

"You mean a hundred marks?" asked Gloster.

"Dollars!" Hendriksen said promptly.

"Well, a hundred dollars . . . I guess I haven't any right to refuse that much," said Gloster, with an embarrassed laugh.

"Then come with me," urged Hendriksen. "We'll start

16

right now."

"Where to?"

"The Linkhorn road."

"I'll just roll my things together and pay my bill. It doesn't matter particularly to me what direction I head in. Just wandering around, you know," said Gloster.

In fact, he had his bag in the car five minutes later when Hendriksen ran down the front steps and waved goodbye to the proprietor. A moment later the exhaust was purring and they slid away into the brightness of the moon and the shadows of the hills.

"What's your line, Gloster?" asked Hendriksen.

"Well, I only kind of travel around," said Gloster, uneasily. "I'm fixed with a little money. It won't take me a step at home but over here with the tourist mark I get along pretty swell."

Something made Hendriksen ask, "Where'd you get the words you were passing to that girl to the tune of 'Anyhow'?"

"Why a friend of mine made them up," said Gloster more brightly. "Pretty, don't you think?"

"Yes, rather," agreed Hendriksen, his suspicion lulled at once. He began to dream of fjords, of the little fishing boats and the incredibly long, bright days of the Norwegian summer.

They shot down the side of a lake, frosted over with moonlight except for one mountain shadow which carved a bite out of the shining silver. The echo of the exhaust rattled among the white pillars that flanked a bridge.

"Better take that left turn," suggested Gloster.

"That's not the Linkhorn road," said Hendriksen.

"I guess it's our road, though." said Gloster, putting the muzzle of an automatic on the crook of Hendriksen's right arm.

17

The Norwegian took the left turn. He could only say, "How great a fool have I been?"

"Not so very great," said Gloster.

"Were you the one who put the motor out of shape?"

"No, a friend did that before me."

The road was winding swiftly among the trees, a mere lane among the mountains. "No, you're not a fool. Maybe just a little young, but time will take care of that," said Gloster. "You wouldn't think of piling this car up against one of these trees, would you? Because there'd be a bullet through you the first twist you gave the wheel. . . . Sorry I've got to talk like this. . . . You can ease her up here and turn off the road into that field."

The mountains had opened their arms a trifle. To the left of the road, behind a fringe of trees, stretched the level brightness of a small meadow. Hendriksen turned the car for it, as a thin drone of sound cut into the field of stars high above them. Gloster instantly switched off the lights of the car, which swept at that moment under the shadows of the trees. It seemed to Hendriksen that he understood his companion's thoughts. In fact the Germans were sure to be on the watch. Those eyes in the sky might be looking for him since he had disappeared from Grossenhain. He stopped the car at Gloster's signal.

CHAPTER THREE

HENDRIKSEN LAY at the foot of a tree with small wires binding his arms and legs. It seemed to his excited mind that the tree was all of silver moonlight, growing up toward the song of a violin in the sky, among the stars. That was the airplane, ripping the sky apart like a knife with a dull edge. In the distance, somewhere among the hills, the siren of an official automobile shrilled as small as a cricket. That sound was his friend, and so was the drone of the airplane overhead. Everything official in Germany was his friend.

The American was standing beside him. "You've got nice eyes," said Gloster. "Sort of gray and green. You remind me of a girl I used to know back in Wyoming. Or was it Denver?" said Gloster. "You can't be very dirty even if you're in this game. Will you tell me where the stuff is?"

Hendriksen looked up quickly at the stars.

"I ought not to leave you behind me alive," said Gloster. "But I will if you'll play the game with me. Will you tell me where you got the Maginot plans, and where they're hidden in the car? If you will, I'll leave you here by the car. They'll find you before long. They're hunting you now."

The siren of the official automobile sounded again, either nearer or with a favoring wind behind the sound. Hendriksen said nothing. He looked at the beautiful, silver poplar.

"Tell me where the stuff is," Gloster urged.

"I don't sell myself twice," said Hendriksen.

"You don't— well," said Gloster. "Then I've got to say goodbye to you."

"All right," said Hendriksen. He looked at the gun that Gloster took from his coat.

"You won't change your mind?" asked Gloster.

"No," said Hendriksen, and closed his eyes. His muscles turned into hard rubber as he waited.

The powder would burn the flesh of his temple. The skin would furl back at the wedge of the wound, scorched away. He saw, in his mind, how the wound would be. But what he saw more clearly was the dipping and the winding of the school road, near home, frozen white most of the year, and the school stuck on the side of the hill. In that funny little school, he had been brighter than the rest. Now he had found that you can't be so bright and win. It makes you different from other people. Somehow, he always knew and could always answer, just as he had now. Nobody could argue with him about it. A man can't sell himself twice.

It was not a gun that spoke, at last. It was Gloster. He said, "Well, all right. You win."

Hendriksen opened his eyes. When he turned his head, he could see Gloster in the automobile, a vague form.

"How can we find anything without a flashlight?" asked a girl's voice. "Shall I get one from the plane?"

That was the girl, speaking English now with a distinctly upper-class accent.

"We'll have to use our sense of touch," said Gloster. "Try to feel or to hear the crackle of paper under the leather. A light won't help us."

20

Lifting his head against the trunk of the tree, Hendriksen glanced over the sparkle of brush and the watery sheen of grass that filled the meadow. A queer shape stood on the verge of the shadow beneath the trees on the farther side of the field. He made out a tiny low-wing monoplane that looked too small to hold one man, to say nothing of two.

From the windings of the hill road, the siren of the official car snarled and whined as it came straight for them. The car still gleamed on the road not fifty yards away. It looked like a slice cut out of a streamlined battleship, a turret on wheels; and it went so fast that it was more of a sound than a sight; then it leaped out of view.

"Peekaboo," said Gloster, laughing.

Hendriksen said nothing. Sweat and moonlight filmed his face with a bright oil; he kept his mouth open and panted like a mountain climber. Gloster's dark form did not seem to move inside the open car. Then a winged shadow fled over the brightness of the meadow twice as fast as a hawk ever flew; a wedge of darkness and light shot at the trees across the clearing and whipped away over the tops of them. Afterward the roar of the plane rattled into Hendriksen's ears.

"We've got to go, Willie!" cried the girl. "They've spotted us. If we could see them, they could see us."

"Maybe," said Gloster.

"I'm going to start the engine now!" she said.

"No. I don't think so," Gloster said.

The siren of an automobile squawked in the hills not far away, like one long word of comment on his remark.

"They're coming back. The car is coming back!" said the girl. "The plane has spotted us and signaled them—telephoned—Willie! You hear me?"

"Gag Hendriksen but don't choke him. Know how to do it? We can't have him shouting to them."

She ran to Hendriksen and balled his handkerchief into a knot. "I'm sorry!" she said. Her hands were cruelly strong, like the hands of a man, as she forced it into his helpless, unwilling mouth.

"I've got it, I guess," said Gloster from the car. "Pasted or sewed inside this seat's upholstery. Think of riding on top of Maginot's brains, will you?" There was a sound of leather ripping under a sharp knife. "Get the plane!" called Gloster.

The girl ran. Gloster came over to Hendriksen, still gathering up the folds of stiff paper under his arm.

"Before I go," said Gloster, "I want to tell you that I'm sorry for you, Hendriksen." He pulled the gag from Hendriksen's mouth. "You were sold out."

"Did he sell me?" groaned Hendriksen. "Did that dog Cailland sell me out?"

Gloster stuffed the gag back between the Norwegian's teeth. Then the siren of the automobile yelled out not far away, the sound prolonged to an endless scream of the echoes. Gloster ran for the plane. Into the dimness beside the monoplane he disappeared.

The screeching voice of the car shot out of the ravine where it had been stifled, left the mist of its own echoes behind, and blared in the open. The brakes groaned, pulled it to a halt on the nearest curve of the road. Not a searchlight but a flash bulb of enormous power flared strongly enough to drown the moonlight and blind Hendriksen's straining eyes.

By the time the trembling shadow had cleared from his vision five men had issued from the car, four of them with heavy guns under their arms and the fifth a big fellow with a walking stick. He pointed with his stick and the four broke into a run straight toward the motionless monoplane beyond Hendriksen.

Its motor roared at the same moment, an unexpected volume of sound, like a man's voice from a small boy's throat; and the plane slid out slowly from the shadow into the silver of the moonshine. The rough of the ground dipped its wings to this side and that; the pudgy little wheels left black trails in the dewy brightness of the grass. The four gunmen ran past Hendriksen. One of them almost tripped over him, plunged on.

Three of them dropped to their knees; one pitched flat on the ground; and all their guns opened like a chorus of rivet-drills on a steel building. The monoplane wavered, veered, turned straight for the marksmen with gathering speed. The whirling propeller was a disk of shining mist in which a highlight swayed from side to side. The gun fire ceased. The four men scattered as the plane swept at them. They were on the ground again in a moment as it went by, the wing tip not ten feet from Hendriksen. Already it was traveling so fast that he heard the small song of the struts in the air.

A bank of trees lifted in front of it. The heart of Hendriksen lifted with it; and yet half his hope was with the fugitives. Through the uproar of the motor came sharp, tinkling sounds, like hammers on thin metal, as bullets ripped through the monoplane. The four guns rattled without ceasing.

The monoplane left the ground. It hung like a bright bird for an instant against the dark wall of the trees. If it crashed, there could be no hope for its occupants at that speed . . . and if the plans could be saved from the wreckage—if only flames did not wrap the plane at once . . . sixty-thousand dollars. . . .

Nothing showed against the trees, now. But a silver bird flew away over the tops of them. The thunder of the motor grew dim all at once.

"See if Hendriksen is dead," said the man with the walking stick.

The four lifted him to his feet and untied the cords that bound him.

"He lives, Excellenz . . ." said one of the brown shirts.

"I have told you before," said the dispassionate voice, "that my name is Ludwig von Emsdorf. There is only one Excellenz in Germany, today, and he chooses to be called by another name. . . . Hendriksen, are you badly done in?"

"I'm not hurt."

"What luck!" said von Emsdorf. "What luck that they didn't bash your head in for you instead of wasting such precious time, such invaluable seconds, tying you and leaving you as a witness behind them!"

A train of whining sound drew across the sky; a monoplane flashed above the trees and disappeared in the direction of Gloster's flight. Von Emsdorf followed this flash of speed with a single casual lift of his eyes.

"Better sport than hawking," said von Emsdorf. "But they'll soon have that heron down."

A chorus of motors roared suddenly out of the sky. Over the edge of the trees came Gloster's monoplane again, gliding low.

"Ah!" said von Emsdorf. "Do you see? Clever fellow, he managed to dodge back through them. But they'll have him soon, I dare say."

Well above Gloster hung two pursuit planes, still climbing into a surer position of advantage, like two hawks mounting above one quarry. One of them dipped down as the shadow of Gloster whipped across the meadow. The noise of the machine gun could not be distinguished from the crackling of the motors, but the heavy rain of lead

24

spattered on the ground.

Gloster's plane dodged, swerving with the downward wing tip almost among the top branches, while the German rebounded to be ready for another pounce. His fellow turned over and came down through the moonlight in beautiful style. The tracer bullets felt for the target with ghostly fingers and found it before all three planes disappeared beyond the trees again.

"Outnumbered, without a machine gun, in an inferior plane, he won't last long," said von Emsdorf. "But he flies well, doesn't he?"

The crackling roar of the motors came vaguely to them out of the distance. Right up against the moon was a flicker of shadow and brillance; three gleams of speed that crossed the face of the moon and dissolved in the translucent fleece of a cloud.

"How the devil has he managed to get up that high?" asked von Emsdorf, but he spoke without anger, patiently, as one sure of his game.

Chapter Four

THE GREAT presses and the machinists who run them seem the important part of a metropolitan newspaper in America; the little patter of typewriters somewhere above appears to mean nothing. But in Paris the paper is cheaper, the ink more acrid, dust lingers for a decade at a time, and the writers have a certain significance.

Jules Cailland appreciated that significance since for three days the inner sanctum of the editor-in-chief of *La Liberté* had been turned over to him. It was his bedroom, dining room, and study. He had a cot in the corner; and when he sat down to his typewriter he felt the world like a million thin ghosts leaning eagerly over his shoulders.

Outside, a Parisian rain dirtied the city, and the lights were on along the streets an hour before their time; but inside his chamber Cailland felt the sun of importance shining on him so steadily that his heart was warmed. He was arranging his notes for the third installment of his revelations and he was almost ready to sit down to the typewriter when the editor-in-chief came in.

He was a plump little man. The war had left him with a limp that had destroyed for him all possibility of physical activity, so that he was oversize in all directions, with a red vein of Burgundy running untapped at one side of his nose. No one around *La Liberté*'s office had ever seen him without a sheaf of papers in his hand, and he waved half a dozen sheets at Cailland now. Cailland sat back from the typewriter, big, blond, heavy with strength like a horse, but with that Norman look of agility in spite of his weight.

"Even Japan!" said Monsieur Grevaux. "Even Japan is asking the serious consideration of the government; it wants the *exposé* of Jacquelin to stop. That Jacquelin, has he stretched his arms all around the world? What a devil!"

Cailland rubbed the thick back of his neck and looked up at the ceiling. "Yes," he decided, "yes, a devil!"

"Give up the photograph this time, Jules," said Grevaux. "We can't keep the world on tenterhooks forever."

"The more they expect the more they will read," said Cailland. "And I can write out twenty articles like the ones that have come."

"Twenty? My dear Jules, you say you were with him only a year?"

"He's like a boiling pot," said Cailland. "He's never still. New things come up to the surface every moment when one is with Monsieur Jacquelin."

"Tell me one thing," said Grevaux. "He is French?"

Cailland considered. "Pardon me," he said. "Not even to you, my dear friend; it might be dangerous, even to you, if you knew."

"Perhaps you're wise," said Grevaux. "And Jacquelin himself? Is it to be the end of him?"

"Well, judge for yourself," said Cailland. "A dozen countries are clamoring to stop the articles. And once Jacquelin is exposed, every one of the dozen will have to put him out of the way lest he fall into the hands of an enemy and be pumped dry of everything he knows! No, he will have to die. Of course."

"Ah, Cailland, you pity him? You still love him?"

"I can't think of that," said Cailland. "Once I've begun, I have to carry on to the end. Unless I account for him now, he will surely account for me."

A voice said at the door, "A telephone call for Monsieur Cailland. Will you take it, monsieur? It is long distance. From Alsace."

Cailland picked up the instrument. A girl's voice said, "Monsieur Cailland?"

"It is I," said Cailland. "Who is speaking?"

"A friend," said the girl, "and I am calling to tell you that you are in danger of your life, monsieur."

"So are we all, my dear," said Cailland. "In danger from whom?"

"Hendriksen failed," said the girl's voice. "He was intercepted and the plans were taken from him. It is known that he got them from you. The price is known. The ministry will be reaching out its hands for you at once. Be swift, monsieur. And adieu!"

Cailland sat for another moment with the receiver pressed hard against his ear; but the voice no longer lived upon the wire and the empty humming sent through Cailland's powerful body a thrill, ice cold.

"Monsieur, I must be alone," said Cailland. *"Seul,"* he repeated, heavily.

Grevaux went softly through the door and closed it behind him. Outside, he said to his secretary, "Poor Cailland! A sorrowful stroke of some sort. Poor, poor Cailland! The telephone is a wretched thing."

In a few minutes Cailland came out with a thick portfolio under his arm. He still was white and moved his lips as though he were trying to bring moisture into his throat; and his eyes fixed straight before him. "I must go out for

28

a few moments."

"Monsieur! Jules!" cried Grevaux. "Leave the building? Adventure into the open street? *Mais vous êtes fou, mon cher.* It is insane to think of such a thing. . . . Jacquelin! Think of Jacquelin! Jules, what is in your mind?"

"Au nom du bon Dieu, don't question me," said Cailland, and walked straight down from the office to the street.

The secretary of Grevaux came from Gascony, where wits are so sharp that the hunter reads the mind of the bird and knows on which bush it will alight. He had looked full into Cailland's face and he said, as the big man disappeared, "He will never return. The road he sees has no turns in it! And you see that he had his papers under his arms?"

"True!" said Grevaux. "My God, if he should not come back—if the articles. . . . Ah, *quelle catastrophe.* Georges, take your coat and hat and follow him. Quickly! Quickly!"

But when Georges reached the street, a great gust of wind and rain blinded his eyes. His heart sank. He turned into the river of wet people who hurried up the pavement and . . . took the wrong direction.

Cailland had gone the other way. He had no raincoat but he did not feel the rain that pressed down the brim of his hat with its weight. He walked stiffly, for a square or two, until the first coldness of terror left him; after that he went through the crowd like a hunting dog through tall grass. He had no objective except to get far from his starting place. As for the rest of the world, it seemed a cramped little place in which one hardly could spread one's elbows. In the old days of gold, a man could step onto a ship and disappear from the ken of the rest of the nations for two or three years at a stretch; but steam and the airplane have shrunk our original dimensions. Cailland yearned with all his heart for a greater globe, an endless space, or some lost island in the sea, unvisited by any ship.

In the speed of his walking he felt some relief, putting the crowd roughly behind him, with a sense that they were swirling like leaves in the wind behind his ample shoulders. And then it seemed to him that one of those leaves was not drifting away but held inside the wind of his own traveling.

He checked his speed a little and looked over his shoulder. At the same time the man from the rear came up beside him. Cailland halted and laid a hand against the wet wall of the building.

"Jacquelin!" he said.

"Walk on," said Jacquelin.

"Jacquelin, in heaven's mercy!"

"Walk on."

Cailland walked on. A bridge across the Seine humped its back not far away. And the rain breathed down upon Paris like a foul gray smoke.

A Londoner loves his city as a sailor loves his ship because he sees it surviving so much bad weather, and this was a typical London day with the rain vainly trying to wash the air clean and depositing the soot of its labors in the laps of the citizens. Most Londoners have learned to accept electric light as cheerfully as sunshine but Winton Holling Jones felt no happiness as he turned his back, for a moment, on the Great Man who was the guest of his office, this afternoon, and looked over the brown, slowly-changing face of the Thames.

Winton Holling Jones had special reasons for happiness at that moment but the fact was that he had lost the habit of happiness years before; and whenever he looked into his own mind or whenever he stared out the window of his office he saw the problems of the Empire stretching before him like a mental blueprint.

Not the Great Man, but the telephone, called him back to his desk. He listened for a moment and hung up. Then he relaxed in his chair.

"They're safely down on Croydon Field," he said, "and they've started on in an automobile. They won't be here for forty-five minutes, if you want to put in that time at another place."

The Great Man rose. Then he sat down again.

"I'll wait," he said. "You're bringing them in with a strong escort, of course?"

Winton Jones seemed to forget the question. He took off his glasses and rubbed his tired eyes, and then he passed his hand on over the big dome of his head. He was not fifty but his hair was a thin white mist.

His visitor showed no irritation on account of this delay. His own position was very high but it might be very temporary, whereas this little man with the great skull had continued for decade after decade at the head of the secret service of His Britannic Majesty. Of his own agents, only the most distinguished ever saw his face; perhaps there were not twenty people in the Empire who knew that the mysterious Mr. R. who was the secret ear and eye of England was also little Winton Holling Jones. But the Great Man in his office knew well enough and therefore sat with consummate patience to wait for an answer to his question about the escort.

"There are three cars traveling in front of the automobile which is bringing them through the city. Two more cars go behind them," said Holling Jones. "There are four men in each automobile. Yes, I think they are fairly well escorted."

"Jones," said his visitor, "how could you dare to do it? How could you dare to turn to a woman in such a pinch?"

"When I'm desperate, Meredith," said Winton Jones, "I generally turn to a woman. Usually I know the highest and lowest brackets inside which a man can work, but I never can tell what a woman may be able to do; I never know her stretch and reach."

"A very neat idea," said Meredith. He consulted his inward soul and his eye brightened suddenly. "A very neat idea," he repeated. "And this time it worked beautifully. Amazing, though. The fact is that I know Lady Cecil. Exquisite girl. But how on earth could anyone except Winton Jones suspect that she had this in her?"

"Ah, she didn't have it in her," said Jones, "but she found a man for the job."

"What man?"

"I don't know. An American."

"Extraordinary people, the Americans," said Meredith. "So far away, you know."

"Yes," said Jones. "Very far. Very extraordinary."

"And so many of them."

"Yes. So very many," sighed Mr. Jones.

"Buildings seventy floors high. Fancy!"

"Quite," said Jones, never looking outward from his own thought. There was a pause; then he spoke his thought aloud. "Have you some ribbons and medals in the next room to meet her?"

"Ribbons and medals?" said the Great Man.

"Generals and all that," explained the soft voice of Jones. "She has performed a service of the very first magnitude—to England."

"You want a reception committee?"

"Yes."

"Really?"

"Really," said Jones.

"If I may use the telephone . . ."

"Pray do."

"But when using the military some sort of ceremony, as a rule . . ."

"There will be tea," said Jones, dryly.

Mr. Meredith went to the telephone. He had it in mind to argue the point, but after all, what is tea if not a ceremony, when you come right down to it? It hardly can be called a meal, can it?

"Am I to tell them why Lady Cecil is to be honored?" asked Meredith.

"Certainly not."

"No, certainly not," said Mr. Meredith. "They simply will see that honor is being done."

"Naturally."

"Quite," said Meredith, and began his work while Jones opened a small note book and wrote in it with a very fine hand.

When the telephoning ended, Winton Holling Jones said, "Perhaps it would be as well if I received her alone, here, in the first place. Then I can bring her to you and the rest in the next room? You may tell them that they have just happened in—called to the war office on official business—they only know that Lady Cecil has performed an extraordinary service, brilliant and heroic. They are not stupid enough to ask questions, of course."

"Official—extraordinary—stupid—of course," said Meredith, making mental notes aloud; and he left the room.

That was why Lady Cecil was ushered into the little office with its iron filing cabinets marching all around the walls, shoulder to shoulder, and found only little Winton Jones. She had known him for a long time. He was in fact an obscure friend of her father and she knew in a dim way that he was connected with the secret service; but she had expected to be received by someone of more importance because of what she carried in the fat briefcase under her arm.

"Oh, it's you, Mr. Jones?"

"No, it is not I," said Winton Jones, smiling.

She stared at him for a moment, remembering the still, small voice which had spoken to her over the wire from London to Paris.

"Ah, but you're not . . ." she began.

"Certainly not," said Winton Jones, still smiling.

But the truth had flashed in her eyes and dazzled her. To how many other agents in the entire empire had Mr. R. unveiled himself? Already, she felt, she had her reward, a strange breath of glory and power that left her in a dream. Before she recovered from it, Winton Jones had spread out the rolls of paper, held them flat with paperweights, and was poring over them with the dreaming eyes of a poet.

"Beautiful!" he said, from time to time. "Very, very beautiful!"

"But everybody," said Lady Cecil, "knows exactly where the Maginot Line runs. Everybody knows who cares to. It can be photographed from the air. Why is it so important?"

"Did you ever see a wasp sting a caterpillar, my dear?" asked Jones, holding his place on the charts with a long, pale forefinger, while he lifted his gentle eyes to her. He took off his glasses so that he could see her beauty more clearly; it was for close work that his eyes betrayed him.

And he smiled for him as she answered, "I never saw a wasp sting a caterpillar."

"The point is," said he, "that the caterpillar has a nerve center in each segment of its body and the wasp that wants to preserve it for the larva has to poison the sections one by one. Oh, very precisely. A fine surgeon could not be more

34

exact. The sting finds the brain of every segment, exactly, and the whole caterpillar is then in cold storage for the larva's diet. . . . You don't mind these gruesome details, Lady Cecil?"

She looked thoughtfully at him and shook her head.

"The Maginot Line is like a caterpillar," he went on. "It is not one continuous covered trench, no matter how deep. . . . It is interrupted here and there. There are isolated portions, you see? And here and here and here are the main reservoirs for manpower. Some of these levels are almost a thousand feet below the surface. Suppose that the German army—let us say—wanted to strike across the great Maginot Line, how happy their high command would be to know the great nerve centers, and sting them to death, and so pass on through the breach! The nerves themselves are indicated on these master charts. You see where the electric wires run? Electricity is the life of the system, of course. Electricity lifts the great elevators. Electricity has to run the underground trains.

"With this chart in hand the Germans could anatomize the Maginot lines. They could paralyze them with a few delicate, precise touches, and then operate on the senseless body. . . . And those are a few of the reasons why we were a little troubled when we thought of the plans in German hands. Shall I tell you some more?"

"Please," said the girl.

"Suppose then that Italy and Germany together push out for elbow room—how Italy would enjoy a slice of Algiers, for instance—they would not be striking like men in the dark if they had this beautiful chart of the Maginot Line. Instead, they would have the sun over their shoulders, shining in the faces of the French . . . but that brings me back to you, Lady Cecil. What shall I say to make you happy? What shall I say to express my gratitude?"

35

"Just a little bit of surprise," said she, "would be worth tons of praise."

She watched his face and laughed before he smiled.

"It was William Gloster—really," she said. "He did it all. Nearly every bit. Once he used me like bait on a hook. That was about the only way I helped."

"Do you expect me to praise the tool more than I praise the workman?" asked Jones, shaking his big head. "I can't do that, you know."

"But if you had seen him!" said the girl. "We had to go south to get away from the two planes. They were faster than we. Their machine guns will never stop—in my brain. But somehow we got into the mountains. Willie took us around the corners of ravines like a roller coaster. Once I looked back and saw one of their planes smash against the side of the cliff we'd just dodged. It seemed to stick there against the rock for a moment, like a bit of sticky mud. And then it fell. Not the plane. You couldn't see the plane. Only streams and lumps of fire dripping down through the air. . . ."

"Ah, good girl!" said Jones.

"What on earth did I have to do with it? I'm telling you how William Gloster flew his plane and how we got away. Everything was as smooth as could be—at least, until we ran out of gas and cracked up near Paris."

"And we'll have to pay for that plane, I dare say," sighed Jones. He began to collect the portions of the great chart, stacking them.

"If they gave him another plane made of gold and set with diamonds, it wouldn't be enough!" said Lady Cecil.

"But he's only an American."

She looked at him and fortunately saw that he was smiling.

"And he only did it for you," said Jones. "I've heard

about William Gloster, of course. He likes to shoot lions, doesn't he? And he's flown over Everest, and he even can talk to bushmen in Australia, I've been told."

"You think he's only a playboy, don't you?" asked the girl.

"My dear, don't we all wish we could play games as he does and always win? Because if he didn't win, he'd be dead, wouldn't he?"

"Yes. Yes, he would. Will you promise me one thing?"

"Anything!" said he.

"Suppose that this last adventure should give him a taste for more of the same kind. You won't give him an opportunity, will you?"

"I'm sorry," said Jones.

"You mean that you'd break your promise?"

"Instantly," said he.

She had begun to breathe deeply in her anger until she saw how weary and pale and old he was. "You know," said Lady Cecil, frowning, "he's not such a silly boy as you take him to be . . . He's made millions in business . . . it's only. . . ."

"Are you going to marry him, Cecil?"

"I don't know," she said.

"I hope not."

She looked sharply at him, full of quick anger and pride.

"My dear, let me assure you of one thing," he said with solemnity. "Whatever I think of Mr. Gloster, I don't think that he's a silly boy. But adventurers who love physical danger—you know they don't live forever, and I was thinking only of your future."

"Ah?" she said, by no means satisfied. "Haven't you the least desire to meet him?"

"Nothing in the world would please me more. Is he in the outer office?"

"He left me here. He wouldn't come in. But he's returning for me later."

"I'll see him then, with much pleasure. Will you take tea with us here while you wait for him to come?"

"Ah," went on Jones, opening the door, "there seems to be a crowd. You won't mind that, will you? Lady Cecil, let me present General Sir Frederick Wister, General Lester Bishop, Colonel the Honorable Peter Standish, Captain Lord Packington, Major. . . ."

And as the introductions ended he whispered to her: "Keep the briefcase, Cecil. I want you to give it, a little later, with your own hands, to the minister for war. . . ."

She felt that she was enthroned. If they did not know exactly what she had done—and certainly there was not the most trifling allusion to the Maginot Line—they seemed to realize that this was an occasion. They treated her, in short, as only English gentlemen know how to treat a pretty girl who is decidedly in the swim.

It was sometime later—she hardly knew when—that old General Wister was saying, "But if you're just from Paris, you know what lies behind *La Liberté*'s last article—the windup of the Cailland series that was to expose Monsieur Jacquelin. Tell us the secret!"

"I haven't even seen today's paper," said she.

"Not seen it?" cried the general. "Not really seen it? Why, it's a tremendous sensation!"

He paused to take breath. She had finished her tea, and a servant picked up her tray from the table beside her and carried it off.

"Sensation, absolutely," said the general, who had regained his breath. "Cailland, in the midst of his revelations, with the whole world gaping for news of this fantastic Monsieur Jacquelin, suddenly disappears. Receives a telephone call and walks out. Absolutely like that. Walks out with his portfolio under his arm and leaves the newspaper strapped. Disappears on the street. Not seen again. Wiped right off the face of the map. Completely lost. . . . And why? Getting good money for his articles. Very good indeed. Has the entire world by the ears. But by Jove, he fades out. *La Liberté* suggests an answer.

"Was it Monsieur Jacquelin himself, who was playing one of his devilish practical jokes on us all? Was he telling just enough truth about himself to tickle the palate and yet reveal nothing of any great importance? In fact, is Jules Cailland the real Monsieur Jacquelin? The newspaper that employed him thinks he is, and it ought to know what it's talking about, oughtn't it?"

A telephone rang and Captain Lord Packington answered it.

"Von Emsdorf?" he said. "I don't know the name. . . . Is there a Mr. von Emsdorf present, please? . . . No?" Packington said into the telephone, "Not here, apparently. . . . Ah? . . . Quite all right!"

"Don't hang up!" shouted Winton Jones, his quiet voice suddenly ringing in the room. "Hold on, will you?"

But Lord Packington already had replaced the receiver. "Pity," he said. "Awful pity you didn't speak a second sooner."

"Didn't you know enough to hold on when a man was talking to you about von Emsdorf?" exclaimed little Winton Jones, rising on his toes to glare at the tall soldier.

"Really—"

"Yes, really!" cried Winton Jones. "You ought to know—you're in a service that ought to know—that von Emsdorf is the top and the crown and the brain and the eye of the German secret service. What did the voice on the wire say? Out with it!"

Some of the lordship melted out of the captain's spine.

"He told me that someone here might be interested to know that von Emsdorf had entered the building and left it only a moment ago. That was all."

Winton Jones turned to Lady Cecil and demanded, in such a voice as no man ever had used to her before, "Have you still got it? You haven't lost it, Cecil, have you?"

"No, no," said the girl. "It's here. . . ." She stretched her hand out to the empty top of the table. "It can't be gone," she cried. "The tea tray was put down on it. . . ."

Chapter Five

When Gloster arrived, he was shown into a room where Lady Cecil sat alone with Winton Jones. She got through an introduction in a halting voice.

Gloster said, simply, "Where's the wash-out, Mr. Jones?"

"Your work," said Winton Jones with equal simplicity, "is gone. Germany has taken back the plans of the Maginot Line."

"Out of my hands," said the girl. "Out of my hands, Willie! Take me away, please."

"You're not saying anything?" said Gloster, looking hard at Winton Jones. "You're not saying that we all have bad luck, now and then?"

Winton Jones, with much point, said nothing whatever.

"Willie, will you go?" whispered the girl.

"I haven't thanked you for your magnificent work, Mr. Gloster," said Jones, "which is the. . . ."

"Speaking of that plane of mine which cracked up," said Gloster, "you won't have to pay for that."

"Ah?" said Jones very pleasantly.

"No," said Gloster, "the important point will simply be to replace it. I'll take one of those little Burleigh-Whitcombe whizzbangs that do two-hundred-and-fifty miles an hour with their eyes closed."

"Is *that* all you want?" murmured Jones.

"It won't come out of your pocket," said Gloster.

"No, but it will come out of my hide, if I may be permitted that expression," answered Winton Jones. "Goodbye . . . Goodbye, Lady Cecil. . . ."

When they got out into the London weather he said, "Where?"

"I don't know, I don't care," said the girl. "I want to die."

"You will, some day," answered Gloster, and put her in a hansom cab drawn by a horse that looked at least half alive. "Slowly, driver," he cautioned.

"Ay, sir," said the cabby, "there's no sense in going whirling along through fine weather."

Gloster looked at the weeping London sky and said nothing. They went clinking off up the street.

"How is it? Bad?" he asked.

"I'm sick," she said.

"Don't be. Not in your English sense," said Gloster. "Want a dash of cold water in the face? I think we're going to have one before long?"

"Have you that damned accordion with you?"

"Yes," he said.

"Then play me something, Willie."

He played her something.

"I didn't mean Scotch caterwauling, either," she said.

He played her a song of Provence—and sang the words close to her ear. They translate somewhat like this:

> Old ocean, I see you stretching your claws;
> I see the white of them unsheathing on the sand,
> And although you pretend to be sleeping,

And although I hear your regular snoring breath,
Still, Father Ocean, I am not deceived.
For the great ships that wander foolishly out from
  shore,
They are the little white mice
That you will have for your dinner.

She tried to laugh a little. "Willie, you're such an idiot,"
she said. "Do you think that's a very consoling song?"

"Shall I try another? What shall I sing about?

"There's another jolly one they sing in Provence," he
said. "Here it goes." And he sang another homely little
tune. It finished with the couplet:

And the wide meadowlands are shining;
But honor, honor, honor is withdrawn from me.

She looked up to him. "Why do you do it, Willie?" she
asked, when he had finished. "Are you trying to break my
poor heart?"

"Hearts don't break," he said. "They're as tough as rubber. Use their toughness when you get in a pinch. Look
at those buildings with the fog and the smoke-water dripping
off their faces. That's the sort of a scene you need when
you're feeling down. You don't want sunshine when you're
blue. That's why Italians are such a gloomy lot. But the
English are so damned merry because there's always more
warmth inside them than there is outside. You always can
cheer up a room with a fire, but air-conditioning is only
a chill up the spine. No, no, De Waters, give me a good,
soggy, dripping, miserable country like England and you'll
find the people singing all day long. And when your heart is
about to break, as you think, go out and wallow in the mire
and see how much blacker it is than you are. All at once
you'll be glad that you're alive."

There was a long moment in which neither of them spoke.

"You have such a funny sort of a mind, Willie," she said, finally. "You know what it makes me think of?"

"A grab bag?" he suggested.

She sat up. "How did you know I was going to say that?" she asked.

"Don't you know why?" he asked.

"We won't go into that," said Lady Cecil. "But Willie—"

"That Winton Jones is a cold in the head, isn't he?" asked Gloster.

"I want to say something, Willie."

"Two cold-hearted devils like Winton Jones would bring down the temperature of the whole nation," said Gloster.

"Willie, will you listen to me?"

"I'd rather look at you."

"Willie. . . ."

"I won't do it."

"You won't do what?"

"Whatever you want me to do. And as far as the Maginot Line plans are concerned, I'm all washed up. I'm through with them. You hear me?"

She nodded. "I want you to go right on and say it all in one swoop," she advised.

"I'm an American," said Gloster. "What do I care about European entanglements? Not a damned thing. The next time you people begin to throw rocks at one another, if you listen toward the west you'll hear a funny noise on the wind. It will be America having its long laugh.

"Listen to me, Europe: We're through with you. No more money. Not a penny. As far as France goes, Germany can have her and welcome. Maybe it would be better that way. Maybe it would be better if all of Europe were just one big country. Then you little nations might make some sense. As it is, you don't. So don't talk Maginot Line to me. The plans can go to the devil. I hope *der Führer* has them now. I hope he's sharpening his nails and filing his teeth to points."

She sat closer to him. "Here's my hand under the robe," she said. "Willie look at me!"

"In another ten years," said Gloster, "you'll be getting toward middle age. You'll weigh a hundred and forty, and you'll have an opinion for every pound you weigh. I pity the man who gets you, De Waters. He might as well marry a radio or an automatic phonograph. You're going to talk all the time about your adventures around the world. You'll tell how the Emir of Turkestan kissed your hand and how the Maharajah of Balderdash gave you the big ruby that was unflawed until the damned footman dropped it. I see your whole life spread out in front of me like a Yorkshire moor, and I don't like it."

"Kiss me, darling," said Lady Cecil.

"Right here in a London street?" he asked.

"Damn London," said Lady Cecil.

"I will kiss you for that," said Gloster, and he did. "We'll drink to the same idea, as soon as we get to an eating place. We'll go to that Maison Basque, God bless it. Half their wines are still unspoiled. De Waters. . . ."

"Yes?"

"Will you marry me tomorrow?"

"Yes, or the day after," she said.

"If there were any faith or truth or honor in you," said Gloster, "that remark would make me a happy man. But there isn't any faith or truth or honor in you, is there?"

"No," she answered.

"Well, that's that," said Gloster.

"Yes," said she. "Will you help me?"

"Damn the Maginot Line and all its plans!" said Gloster.

"Willie," she said, "will you love me a little and help me?"

"I wish you wouldn't make a damn fool of me," said Gloster.

"Don't you think I'm serious? I'll cry if that would help."

"Stop it, De Waters. Will you stop it?"

"All right. I'll stop it."

"What do you want me to do?"

"Take me back to France."

"We'll have to be married first or that would raise a hell of a scandal."

"Will you take me back to France?"

"I suppose so," said Gloster.

"And find Jules Cailland for me."

"What do you want with that handsome piker?"

"Do you know who he is? He's Monsieur Jacquelin!"

"He's my left foot without a shoe on it!"

"Darling, I tell you that he's Jacquelin! Will you take me to France and help me find him?"

"You won't find him in France."

"Why not?"

"Because he's in London. I saw him today. Turning into the Hotel Blessington. I suppose that's where he's staying. When he saw me, the skunk slipped away into the crowd in the lobby. What do you want with him?"

"Willie, if he's Jacquelin, he's the only man in the world who can help me to get back the Maginot Line plans. And we've got to hurry. Already they have a frightful head start. I wish I'd thought of Cailland at once. Stop the cab. We'll take a taxi. . . ."

Monsieur Jules Cailland sat in a corner of the dining room having his equivalent of tea, that is to say, a half

46

bottle of red Bordeaux, some crusty bread, and a portion of Roquefort cheese. He stood up when he saw them coming and said, "Ah, my dear Gloster!"

"Is that wine worth drinking?" asked Gloster.

"It has just come over," sighed Cailland, "but already there is English in it."

"Have you met Lady Cecil?" asked Gloster.

"I have had that honor."

"Oh, but have we really met?" she asked.

"It was one of those great affairs. You could never remember."

"Perhaps not," she said, doubtfully, surveying his height and his thick blond hair and his handsome, shaggy face. He was taller than Gloster by a good two inches. He asked them to sit down.

"She thinks you're Monsieur Jacquelin," said Gloster, bluntly.

"Mademoiselle—monsieur—but please!" said Jules Cailland.

"I told her that it was nonsense," said Gloster.

"She saw that foolish newspaper," said Cailland. *"N'est-ce pas, mademoiselle?"*

"She's young," said Gloster, "and the English, when they're young, believe everything they read."

"That is charming," said Jules Cailland, "though you haven't a charming intention, my dear friend. Monsieur Gloster," he explained with a smile, "is often rude, but that is because America still has a Great West. And besides, there are so many Americans that one of them always feels that he is a majority. My dear Willie, you forgive me?"

The girl laughed with Cailland. "I'm glad you said that," she declared. "I've wanted to say it for a long time. You see that he doesn't laugh?"

"I'm bored," said Gloster. "You little nations over here —you decadent little people—bah! I will not even laugh at them. Jules, order some more wine."

"Where did you know one another?" asked the girl.

"Waiter!" called Cailland. "Another bottle of wine . . . not this unlucky Bordeaux, but a quart of Pommard—Pommard can endure even English cellars, for a while, as a rule."

"Where did you know one another?" insisted the girl.

"Ah, Cecil, don't go into that," said Gloster. "I've been around the world at lot, in my time, and I've been in some dark corners. You'd hardly believe how dark!"

Jules Cailland picked the insult out of the air with his big hand and blew it away with laughter into the outer spaces. "Ah, how rude!" he said. "But we shall not fight till tomorrow."

"Monsieur Jacquelin," said the girl, softly.

"No, no!" murmured Jules Cailland.

"Don't deny it any longer," advised Gloster. "She's made up her mind. See her eyes shining? She's adoring the whole picture. Your big hulk and your face and above all your mystery . . . De Waters, don't be such an ass!"

"But Jules Cailland at your service, mademoiselle," said the Frenchman, anxiously dwelling on her face.

"Willie please tell him," said the girl, watching Cailland as though that employment drank up all her faculties and left her incapable of speech.

"The master plans of the Maginot Line have been stolen from the French war department," said Gloster.

"Tiens!" whispered Cailland.

The mechanical, rapid voice of Gloster went on, quietly. "Taken to Germany. Recovered. By this English agent. Taken to London. Stolen from her this afternoon."

"By von Emsdorf," said the girl.

"That fox!" said Cailland through his teeth.

"Therefore, they're probably on the way back to Germany now. Or will be soon. By air. I suppose the English are watching every airport. But you can't keep a fellow like this von Emsdorf out of the air, I suppose," said Gloster.

"Monsieur Cailland, will you help us?" said the girl. "I don't want you to donate your time, of course. But the loss of the plans is my fault, and I have plenty of money to pay. You can name . . ."

"Mademoiselle, you forget that I am a Frenchman!" said Jules Cailland.

"Don't be a fool, Jules," said Gloster. "She can pay and she ought to. Name your figure."

"Please!" said the girl.

Cailland, staring at her, drew a great breath. "Mademoiselle," he said, "it is for the safety of France . . . and again, I am a Frenchman. I am in your hands. Make use of me!"

Gloster looked from the big fellow to the shining face of the girl.

"I see it," he said. "A damned romance. Oh, Cailland, no wonder you've never had to work, except on the stage. Shall I leave the pair of you together? Shall I? Well, I'll answer myself. When I come back in half an hour, try to be out of this trance."

He came back, in exactly thirty minutes and found them gone. The waiter, with an English face and a French smirk, came up. "The lady seemed to expect you might return, sir," he said. "She left this for you."

He offered an envelope which Gloster tore open and read:

Dear Old Willie,

In ten seconds I saw that it was he. In ten minutes more I knew that it was he, although he still protests.

49

The wonderful truth now is that he is willing to help me, single-handed. I can hardly believe it. I can hardly believe that once more I shall have a chance to get back what has been lost. But I know that he never fails and therefore I have a high heart. Is it going to trouble you a little because I have gone away with him? I hope you will trouble just a little, but how much for the best this is!

I know my headlong, wild, impulsive Willie Gloster. If just straightforward strength and courage were what is needed, no one could do any more than you, but I'm afraid that this business must be done with craft and hesitation and subtleties that neither of us know anything about. And so I'm glad to leave you behind out of danger. A great master is with me and he will see me safely through. I have the most perfect faith in that. I even wonder how I can be anything but a weight on his hands but he says that I will not be in the way. Is that a polite lie? Perhaps. At any rate, I'm going with him.

Goodbye, my dear. Ten thousand thanks for everything, and above all, for bringing me to him.

Cecil

He put the note in his pocket and looked about him, to the scrawny potted palms and the brown pillars, and the mirrors drinking in the dinginess of the day, for he wanted to remember the place as a general wants to remember the scene of his great defeat.

Chapter Six

Winton holling jones walked home every day to stretch his scrawny legs and fill his cramped lungs with air. At every corner he paused, regarded the traffic, and then crossed the street with caution, just as that mind of his crossed with caution all the traffic of international problems, for it was hard to separate the Winton Jones of ordinary affairs from the Jones who controlled the secret service of his country. He looked upon his dinner plate with the same misty far-sightedness with which he viewed an imbroglio in the Far East.

He had just made one of these corner hesitations and started across the street when a big-stepping man drew up beside him and a voice round and resonant said:

"You can control your own agents, Jones, can't you? They don't go off helter-skelter without your sending them, do they? Then call back Lady Cecil, will you?"

"Gone where?" asked Jones, vainly lengthening his step to match the stride of the other. "Lady Cecil gone where, Mr.—er, Gloster?"

"To hell, I suppose, with Jules Cailland. She thinks that he's Monsieur Jacquelin."

At this Winton Jones halted and put his hand on Gloster's arm and looked up into his face. He glanced up and down the street as though to make sure of their privacy, but though the street was quite empty he merely shook his head and walked on again, more slowly. One might have thought that he suspected the crawling London mist of being a sentient thing, capable of overhearing unguarded remarks.

They entered the park. The trees drifted slowly past them. In the distance the trees stood still, gathering dim mantles of evening. The street lights left wavering yellow water marks along the pavements.

"Gone with Jules Cailland!" said Jones. "Well?"

"Call her back," said Gloster.

"How can I?" asked Jones. "If she has taken to the air with Cailland, how can I call her back? I can't whistle down that bird yonder, you know. Really, I'm not God!"

"Then why do you play His part?" asked Gloster.

"Ah?" said Winton Jones.

"Please don't be so damned English," said Gloster.

They walked on for a time in silence. Afterward, Jones said, "I think I should beg your pardon, Mr. Gloster."

"Granted," said Gloster. "Now about the girl."

"When did she leave?"

"An hour ago."

"She's a headlong creature. I'm afraid they may be in the air already."

"I know that. Call her back! Will you call her back?"

"If I called her, would she come?" asked Winton Holling Jones. "I'm afraid not. If she sees her goal, will she turn from it? If the plans of the Maginot Line which she lost—"

"You were there. It was your fault, not hers," said Gloster.

"Ah, but certainly that's true," admitted Jones. "On the other hand when I see an intelligent, high-spirited, rich girl ready to break her heart to be of service to her country, what a singular man I should be if I opened her eyes."

He gestured elegantly.

"Will you look at it another way?" said Gloster. "She's a clean-bred girl but she's been raised in a rotten century where the women no longer give their hands with their hearts but with their brains. She thinks that Cailland is Monsieur Jacquelin. The thought may sweep her off her feet. Do you follow me?"

"I follow you. Unwillingly, I follow you."

"You have long arms. Will you call her back?"

"How shall I find her?"

"If I find her, will you make sure that she has to return?"

Winton Jones took six long steps while he measured this request. Then he said, "Yes—I shall."

Gloster held out his hand. "That's a gentleman's agreement."

Winton Jones regarded the hand. He looked up into Gloster's grim, half-ugly face and then took the hand with a sudden gesture.

"Yes, my dear fellow. Yes, yes!" he said. "But will you go after her? Are you going to jump into the fire again?"

"I am," said Gloster. "Which way shall I jump to find it? Von Emsdorf is the thief. He has the stuff. Will he take it straight to Wilhelmstrasse? Is that where I have to go?"

"No," said Jones. "Not there."

"Where, then?"

"I don't know."

"You have something in mind," insisted Gloster. "What is it?"

He had to wait again while the nervous feet of Winton Holling Jones put another stretch of the black pavement behind him.

"Why should you go at all except with your eyes open?"

asked Jones.

Gloster said nothing.

"There is a cabal," said Jones. "And von Emsdorf is part of it. He may be the guiding brain of it. Perhaps he is. I think he is and I think he stole the Maginot Plans twice to serve an end that was as much personal as national—as much international as national. Let me sketch everything briefly from the beginning. A good deal of it you know already. But let me think aloud."

"Please do," said Gloster.

"Germany is desperate," said Winton Jones. "A few facts prove that. She has less than two million unemployed, within a half million of the best figure since the war. But she's employed her people making war munitions. She's paying them with her blood. I'll give you some figures. Experts in 1929, thirteen billion marks. This year, four billion. The gold Reichsmark costs too much. Foreign trade is dying. But she has to buy raw products—tin, copper, silk, rubber, manganese, chromium, tungsten, textiles, iron ore, and so forth. She has to have nickel for war material. She's trebled her purchases of it. She works like a madman, day and night. She makes substitutes—sugar from wood, flour from potatoes, gasoline from coal, margarine from coal. It turns the stomach to think of what German patriots will have to eat during the next war! But how, with a failing foreign trade, can she afford to pay for her enormous imports? How can she carry on an arms program that costs her four thousand million dollars a year?

"The cleverest financial juggler in the world controls the purse strings—Dr. Schacht. What does he do? Well, he draws 'voluntary' contributions. The bank clerk gets two hundred and ninety Reichsmarks a month, but fifty he pays back as 'contributions.' That helps, but poor Schacht is still in the fire. He gets internal loans that are forced loans.

Last summer, the banks gave him five hundred million marks. The insurance companies gave him three hundred million marks. But he can't get that from them again, and he knows it. They are bled white. In return they have IOUs from the government which, in case of a crash, will mean exactly nothing.

"And while he struggles like a devil to find more money, the air ministry's budget under Goering goes up by two hundred million Reichsmarks for the year! That's the financial background. You see what it means? Germany is arming herself, but she is paying with her blood. Presently there will be no more money left in the national veins. You follow?"

"I follow," said Gloster. "And she feels that she must fight or die."

"Exactly," said Jones. "She feels that she is being strangled to death by lack of room. Her birth rate is actually decreasing. It's estimated that her population in fifty years will be under fifty million as against sixty-five million today. Are Germans going to sit still while fifteen or twenty millions of them vanish from the face of the earth? I don't think so. So Germany rushes on her preparations. She feels a religious eagerness. Hitler says:

" 'In the annihilation of France, Germany sees merely the means of our nation to obtain full development in another direction. Our foreign policy will only have been correct when there are two hundred and fifty million Germans, not crowded like coolies in a factory, but free peasants and workers. Almighty God bless our weapons! Judge if we have merited freedom! Lord, bless our combat!' "

"I've read that," nodded Gloster.

"Now we come to the crux," said Jones. "Germany has been arming as fast as she can but she's still far behind in guns of big caliber and in heavy tanks, and such things.

Furthermore, it will be a long time before she is up-to-date in those directions. These big guns cost like the devil—like the very devil, you know. So do the heavy tanks. Line inland battleships, you might say.

"So Germany's preparation lags. There are two opinions among the war-minded in Germany—and the entire nation is really war-minded. A majority of the conservatives want to wait until the preparation is complete. *Der Führer* leads this opinion on. Remember that he is only a great orator. In the war he did nothing as a soldier. He was a corporal at the end of it. His mind runs to words rather than to actions. Therefore he favors delay before the great crisis. But the minority disagrees.

"They see that their preparation is incomplete but they count on the fervor of the people and the war-weariness of the rest of the world. The shame of defeat still makes the blood of every German boil. And with reason, poor devils, for God knows they fought like heroes! But let that go. There are in Germany certain men made of steel who desire to strike now. As their own preparation goes on, they see that other countries around them, richer in gold, will be making still greater preparations. They feel that their chance is as equal now as it ever will be. Leonhardt von Emsdorf is one of these. Steel, all steel. There's not even iron in von Emsdorf. He wants to strike now. And he has enormous influence. With *der Führer,* with Goering, with Colonel-General Blomberg, with von Fritsch. Von Emsdorf has the ear of all of them. Still, he's working to a certain extent with a lone hand. His cabal has to do not so much with other Germans as it has with other countries, for when Germany strikes she wants to involve other nations all around her so that her flanks will be secure as she faces west. Well, does it still make sense?"

"It still makes sense," said Gloster.

"We've known about this cabal for only a short time, but we have the names of his correspondents in certain countries. There is Jacques Louvain in Belgium, Johann Gleich in Austria, the Conte di Parva in Italy, and that queer monstrosity, that great orator and beast, Gregor Raskoi in Russia itself. More than this, we know that on this very day all four of these men have left their own countries and started for Germany. But we don't know their itineraries. Only at one point—Raskoi changes from plane to train at Landsberg, in Prussia, and is passing on through or to Berlin. That seems to indicate Berlin as the meeting point for all of them, but we're not at all sure. But does the picture grow on you?"

"Von Emsdorf opens the meeting," Gloster said. "He tells them that the time to strike will never be better. Italy to strike for more colonies in Morocco or Algiers, Russia to clean up the Baltic nations, the Austrian Nazis to make a great putsch to unite their country with Germany, and Germany itself to pour west on a France that trusts to the Maginot Line—which will be almost non-existent now that the master plans are in German hands. The cabal agrees; vom Emsdorf brings to *der Führer* a practically completed fact. If *der Führer* is not convinced, then perhaps von Emsdorf intends to reach above his head and appeal to the sword of Germany, the disciplined troops of the Reichswehr. And so—a leap at the throat of Europe."

Winton Jones paused. He turned and looked up steadily into Gloster's face. "You seem to know your Europe," he said.

"You can't wander around the world as I do without hearing bits of news, now and then," said Gloster.

"True," agreed Jones, walking on, but with a thoughtful air. "But now that the picture is clear in your mind, what could you do about it?"

"Find out the meeting place of the cabal," said Gloster. He hummed a little senseless tune. *"Kabale und Liebe.* Schiller, you know. Cabal and Love."

"And how will you find out where the cabal is to meet?" Jones asked, ignoring the interpolation.

"Get to Landsberg before Raskoi takes his train and then tail him to the finish of the trip. I can speak Russian."

"And at the finish of the trip?"

"I'll find Lady Cecil and take her back to England by the scruff of the neck," said Gloster. "With your assistance in case of a pinch."

"Is that all you'll do?" asked Winton Holling Jones, in a weary voice.

"Suppose that I get to the spot, what would you have me do?" asked Gloster.

"What would I like to do if I were there in person?" said Jones, dreamily.

"Yes, put it that way."

"I'd try for some means," said Jones, "of killing them off. Not a quick death, you know. Something slow. So that they would have a chance to look around them. And then I'd want them to see me, laughing, not too far away. Laughing, Gloster, and rubbing my hands. And watching them go up in a fine stench of smoke. That's what I'd like, Gloster, so that another ten million men wouldn't have to die, and leave the world poisoned with hate for fifty years."

CHAPTER SEVEN

GREGOR RASKOI threw a bomb when he was fourteen years old, and was sent to Siberia for it. Siberia had only a year to toughen him before the Bolshevik revolution brought him back to Moscow as a boy hero. He lived violently all the time. He served with the Trotsky forces when they were hunting down the White Russians. When he came back as a colonel, he betrayed Trotsky to gain the favor of Lenin, because there was only one great quality in his mind, and that was an ability to know, in advance, who would win the argument. Then he went out as a red-headed headsman for Lenin, being a good deal more savage about it than Lenin ever imagined. He never talked about his deeds of violence. He only laughed about them. Stalin took him over when Leinin died, too busy to know exactly how savage a monster he'd inherited.

He was a whip in the hands of his masters. He grew to be such a great whip that only one person could handle him, and that was Stalin. And even Stalin was dumbfounded by some of his performances. After a while he gave up actual bloodshed except on rare, holiday occasions. He preferred the more delicate work of extracting confessions from those among the accused whom he felt it particularly important to convict. This labor appealed to his more mature talents, as they ripened. The confessions which prisoners make in Russia sometimes amaze the world, but that is because the world does not know that there are such experts as Gregor Raskoi. Gregor Raskoi, in short, was a law unto himself.

He worked chiefly with electricity. He knew how to step up a harmless current that could not cause death but which traveled along the nerves like saw-toothed probes and wound up by jabbing into the brain. You can't resist electric torture. You can't resist it because it destroys your will power at the same time that it puts the body on the rack.

Big men—big, passive, hard-headed Slavs with no more imagination than lumps of wood could not resist the devices of Raskoi. Presently their heads twisted back and they began to scream, monotonously, terribly, with grating shrillness. Raskoi liked that. It was the only sort of music that appealed to him. What he preferred was to take as many as half a dozen and work on them at the same time with the currents stepped up to varying intensities. He could turn a bass into a shrieking tenor just by varying the intensity of the electric shock, and when half a dozen strong men who would have laughed at cannon were all screaming together and making the only sort of harmony that fed the soul of Raskoi, then Gregor would throw back his own head and show his white teeth and the red of his throat as he laughed.

He came to know just how much to give his patients. He would dose a man so well that half an hour later, when the fellow had to appear in court, he still had no more will power than a baby and confessed with tears and sobbings that seemed to be of the utmost contrition. Gregor Raskoi could have made an angel confess that it had stolen its wings.

60

He had specialties. To make a young girl, a pretty thing, accuse her mother of various dreadfulnesses was one of Gregor's principal joys. He could cause a newly married couple, still sick and trembling with the joy of love, to denounce one another in screeching voices before an astonished court.

In short, Gregor made himself invaluable to the Revolution.

After a while he discovered that vodka, though heavenly, was not the only drink in the world. Witih vodka he got himself drunk in an hour or two, and that was too soon; with French red Burgundy he could keep his throat awash a dozen hours at a time before he was done in. He kept himself well drunk more than half the time, and the cost of the Burgundy was often tremendous. His taste improved. Once he drank nothing but Romanée Conti for an entire month and even kings hardly revel so magnificently as that.

Lenin, it is said, once sent for him and remarked: "Gregor, you are a beast."

"True," said Raskoi. "I'm your beast!"

"Your beastliness costs too much," said Lenin.

Raskoi began to travel around in a high-priced limousine with the Burgundy packed in special side pockets. He learned how to knock the neck off a bottle and pour a whole quart down his throat while he was traveling at full speed, but when there was snow on the ground he always squirted out the last mouthful so as to leave a visible peace offering to Mother Earth.

Raskoi had three wives, one after another, but he sent them all away and their children with them.

"Red Burgundy is my wife and my child," he said. "It is also my father and mother. Lenin was only my grand uncle and Stalin is my uncle. There . . . you know all about Gregor Raskoi!"

61

But people did not hate him as much as you might suppose. He had a way of doing big things. Money made no difference to him. Clothes made no difference. He liked the automobile because it went fast. All he wanted was plenty of wine. And when that soured his belly, he freshened his stomach with a pint of vodka and began on the Burgundy again.

He had a bottle of Clos de Vougeot in his hand when Gloster first saw him walking up and down in the station at Landsberg, waiting for the train. There were no guards about him. That was one of the things that the Russian people liked; Raskoi never had bodyguards. He used his own strength instead of hired guns. Once when three of the men he'd tortured set on him in the street, he knocked the heads of two of them together, and let them escape while he strangled the third man with his hands.

He lay down on the dying man and as the swollen tongue thrust out between the teeth, Raskoi kept shouting, "Farther! Farther!" In fact, he feared nothing in the world except Stalin, and him only a little. He used to say, "I will be a dog to only one man."

That was why he was walking up and down the station with his bottle of Burgundy, unguarded and unafraid. He was about the height of Gloster, and like him he was big with strength. He gave a sign of it while Gloster was watching. He was munching a sausage of fat bacon, and a big street cur came up and begged for a share. Raskoi swung his thick leg and kicked the mongrel away. The dog went off hobbling as though its ribs had been broken. Raskoi laughed and continued his promenade. From time to time he burst into song.

Gloster got out the little pocket accordion and accompanied him. He sang an under part for Raskoi's song—in fact the Russian had a very good voice. It was a little rough and there was too much of it, that was all. Raskoi went up to Gloster at the end of the song and said:

"If you can speak Russian, why do you sing like a damned Frenchman, through your nose?"

Gloster laughed. "I'm still too close to Russia to answer you," he replied.

"Ah," said Raskoi, "you are an émigré, perhaps. You are one of the ones who ran away with your pockets full of rubies and roubles? Is that it?"

"No, but I saw Raskoi and went away. I knew there wouldn't be room for the two of us in one little Russia."

Raskoi was too drunk to understand at once. But when his eyes had swallowed the sense of these words he laughed with his whole heart, like thunder.

"In Berlin," said Gloster, "I could see you."

"Yes, by God, in Berlin!" said Raskoi. "I will make you drunk and it won't cost you a penny. Not a penny. Oh, Saint Catherine, how drunk I shall make you!"

He was still laughing at the thought when the train arrived and they separated and got into it.

The train reached Berlin in the evening, about twenty-four hours after Gloster had said goodbye to Winton Holling Jones. In Berlin people move quickly, like Americans; some of them have big stomachs from beer but most of them are rather pale and their faces are set a little with the strain of labor. But a German, like an American, will pour out his whole life strength rather than decrease his standard of living. The Junkers are that way more than the lower classes; they keep their jaws set almost all the way through life and their eyes are sharply focused on the best chance.

When he got off the train, Gloster found Raskoi no drunker than when he got on it. "Remember," he said, "you are to get me drunk tonight."

63

"Did I say tonight?" said Raskoi. "Well, you come and see me. I'll be at this hotel. You come and I'll get you good and drunk. I'll make wine run into your eyes! If it doesn't run out your ears, I'll keep on pouring it down your throat until it does. You come and get drunk with Raskoi!"

It seemed an immense joke to him. He laughed so that his hand shook as he held out a card to Gloster with the name of the hotel written on it in German script. It was a place on Unter den Linden.

"Come at ten," said Raskoi. "I don't begin to drink well till ten. I only have little drinks before ten, but then I have it by the bottle."

Gloster went off through the long, straight streets of Berlin and looked sadly at the rococo buildings of an earlier period, with harsh, faceless slices of modernity crammed in here and there, like fists among dumplings.

Night was coming, and Lady Cecil was somewhere; and Jules Cailland was not far from her.

He went into a restaurant but he could not eat because he kept thinking about Cecil. The blue evening which was rubbed across the window of the restaurant made him dream of the dusk in London through which he had driven with her. Remembering that moment, he could repeat all her words, one by one. He could take them into his own mouth and re-say them. They left a sweetness in his brain, like wine; and they left a sorrow that sank to his heart and made it cold.

He told himself that she was only a woman, like any other woman. She would get middle-aged, like all of them. She belonged to Cailland, Cailland had her. Cailland had made her his woman.

The thought made him so sick that he put his knuckles against his forehead and ground bone against bone. But even when his eyes were closed, the memory of the girl got inside his eyelids. She shone upon his mind and he knew that that special light never would leave her. Or him. Age would not dim it. She would be beautiful forever.

He sat in the restaurant for a long time, sipping Rhine wine and eating green olives. The wine was iced so that it made his palate ache but the delicate perfumes of it went up into his brain and joined the thought of Cecil, which was lodged there. He was taking the advice he had given to her and was adding sorrow to sorrow, resolvedly, but he could not break down the cold iron that bound his soul. He could not dissolve it by wallowing in regrets.

It came to be ten o'clock and he went to the address of Raskoi but all the way he felt that it was a losing game—that it was too late—that the ruin already had been accomplished. His feet, not his mind, took him to the hotel.

When he tried to telephone to Raskoi's room, the operator said, "You will just have to go up. He has broken the telephone!"

Gloster remembered the weight of the gun which he carried under his armpit. The fact that the telephone was broken seemed to give him an opportunity, in some way. He could not have said exactly how.

When he got up to the door of Raskoi's room, the Russian's thick, rich voice bellowed inside, and he walked in.

Raskoi lay on a couch in the living room. There were some very modern, garish colored prints on the wall of the room. Some of the figures were mere ideas, not images, but Gloster could recognize a blue stallion galloping over the top of a green hill and the sky was a gray background, stippled in. The furniture was comfortable, overstuffed, upholstered in gray, and there was a thick gray rug. It was a good hotel, new in every way. It lacked the *schmack* and smoky old beer flavor of Berlin's more seasoned hostelries.

Raskoi lay on the couch, stripped to the waist with his feet bare, also, though the evening was quite raw.

"Hai, brother!" called Raskoi. "Are you my brother, pig?"

"I am not from the same sty, though," said Gloster.

"You're not from what?" demanded Raskoi, heaving himself half off the couch. He looked like an animal ready to spring from all fours.

"Not from the same sty," said Gloster. "And don't look at me like that."

"How should I look at you?" shouted Raskoi. "I'll break your back!" he yelled and jumped at his guest.

Gloster hit him with all his might on the corner of the chin, so hard that the bone bit into his knuckles painfully. It should have knocked Raskoi right across the room. Gloster had never in his life struck a man with such force. But the blow merely stopped Raskoi's rush and made him take one step back.

"Ah?" he said, and lifted his hand to his chin. His fingers came away with blood on them. "Hai, Elise!" shouted Raskoi.

A girl came into the bedroom door. She was blond as a Prussian and had a pretty, rather delicate face.

"Elise, look!" said Raskoi, and held up his hand with the blood on it. *"He* did it!" said Raskoi. "He did it. That little man. *He* did it to Raskoi."

He began to laugh in a great uproar. "That little man did it to me," said Raskoi. "Shall I kill him?"

"No, don't kill him," said Elise, looking at Gloster, smiling on him.

"All right, I won't kill him," said Raskoi. "He hit me on the chin and I can see my own blood."

He laughed again and hardly could stop his merriment. "Brother," he said to Gloster, "do not get too drunk, because I might strangle you if you fall asleep. Sit down and drink!"

66

There were two cases of Burgundy straw-packed in boxes on the floor. He picked up two of the bottles and knocked their necks off against the radiator. Other bottle necks lay already on the floor.

"Now!" said Raskoi, giving Gloster one of the pair. "Now, deep! Make the last pint splash on top of the first pint."

Gloster drank off the whole bottle. His head rang.

"Give it to me!" said Raskoi. He took Gloster's bottle and held it upside down. No liquid ran out.

"By God," he said, "you must be a Russian, and a noble! Elise! He is a Russian and a noble. Get down on your knees and kiss his feet—down on your knees—"

He lifted his big hand and the girl dropped. Gloster caught her under the armpits and lifted her to her feet.

"He doesn't want you to," said Raskoi, dazed. "He doesn't want you to, by God . . . I won't want you, either. Go get to bed! Be off with you."

The girl disappeared into the bedroom; her dark, slant eyes looked back over her shoulder towards Gloster as she went.

"Now we'll drink," said Raskoi.

He knocked open two more bottles and placed them on the table as he sat down. He was a little fat, but not very. The loose of his belly overhung the top of his belt somewhat and there were some clots of fat under the skin of his neck, but his strength had not yet rotted away.

He sang, and Gloster accompanied him on the accordion. He drank, and Gloster kept pace with him, sweating. He felt that he had to keep pace or else what he meant to do would be more foul and dishonorable. He had to set his teeth and say to himself everytime he took a swallow, "I won't get drunk!" So his will power kept his brain on ice and kept it from getting hot with alcohol.

"I'll tell you a story," said Raskoi, after an hour. "Elise, come in and hear my story."

"I haven't anything to put on," said Elise.

"Come in, damn you," called Raskoi. "If you had anything on I'd tear it off."

She came in wearing a nightgown of thin, pink silk.

"Look at a woman," said Raskoi. "They're all loaded in the hips and gone in the shoulders. If a horse looked like a woman, we'd shoot it to put it out of pain. Look at her! Are you fat inside the knees? No, she's not fat inside the knees. If she was, I would have knocked her over the head. . . . Come here!"

He pulled her into his lap. "Take some of this," said Raskoi.

"Don't cut my mouth," said Elise, holding up her hand for protection from the sharp edges of the broken bottle neck.

He slapped her hand out of the way. "I won't cut your mouth. That would only give you red kisses, you fool," said Raskoi. "I'm going to tell you something. Listen to me."

She lay back in the arms of Raskoi and looked up into his face like a baby, inert, watchful of strange things. Under her blond hair and her blond eyebrows, her eyes were exceedingly dark. The eyelashes were sooty shadows.

"The first time I saw a battle, it was like this," said Raskoi. "I was off with the cavalry on the left wing. I looked across the battlefield. It was nice to see the infantry go on in lines. It was pretty to see the artillery gallop out in front and unlimber. Little puffs of white blooming like white roses. Lovely! Whiter than your throat, sweetheart, and the sky was bluer than this vein—this one that I pick up between my thumb and finger. You see, brother? And we sat up there on our horses, watching. . . . Give me another bottle . . . to war—to fight—there's the sport. I think of men who play tennis and my belly turns over. They could

68

play war, just as well. . . ."

He poured down his bottle of wine. Gloster finished his at the same time and locked his teeth. He was getting drunk. The sudden great floods of the wine half nauseated him. He looked at the girl and her eyes found him at the same time.

"Look at me, you slut," said Raskoi. "I won't have you looking at anything else. If you look at him, I'll kill you both and hang you out the window for the birds to pick at. . . . But I was talking about the first battle . . . Battle . . . I heard a shell whistle in the air, going faster than a bird, and traveling south. . . . I wanted to go south, too— Then a messenger rode up and saluted the squadron commander. He kept his hand at the visor of his cap while he talked. But every now and then he would turn his head a little and spit. I wanted to see the commander stick a sword through him but he only looked and listened. He looked as though he were reading a book. Then I saw that the grass was red. The messenger was spitting blood."

The girl sat up.

"Be still!" said Raskoi, and struck her back into his lap. She lay still. The red marks of four fingers grew out on her cheek. Her eyes turned to Gloster and would not leave him.

"Give me wine! Why the hell is there no wine? D'you think you can steal it?"

Gloster opened two bottles, Raskoi poured down one of them at once. Gloster fought his own bottle down by degrees. He knew that he could not take another.

Raskoi stood up. He was shouting. And he had thrown the body of the girl across his shoulder.

"I said to the messenger: 'Where are you shot?'

" 'Through the lungs,' he said.

" 'You're going to die,' said I. 'You know that? You're going to die.'

"And then something made me laugh at him.

"He spat in my face. He spat all over my face and when

I wiped it away, I saw that it was all red. It was blood. And I laughed. It's only the second time, tonight, that I've had blood in my face—and both times—I laughed—I laughed . . ."

He began to stagger. "I laughed . . ." shouted Raskoi, roaring with mirth. He reeled and fell by the couch. The girl got up from him. Raskoi lay still with his arms and legs spread wide.

"Now!" said the girl. "You can get away!"

Gloster went to the door and stepped out. There was a numbness through his brain out of which a thick voice kept saying to him that he could not harm a drunken man.

He went downstairs through the lobby to the open street. The sweet coldness of the air blew through his lungs. He walked for half an hour, with his knees strengthening and the fumes blowing out of his brain. Then he turned and came back to the hotel.

He was sober enough to know that he must not go back through the lobby into the hotel. He had been seen going out and he must not be seen returning. The room of Raskoi opened on a fire escape, so he went around through the alley behind the building and jumped to catch the lower end of the fire escape. There was enough strength in his arms to pull his body up but when he got to the first steps above, he had to crouch for a moment. His heart was racing so from the effort that he lost his breath and it would not come back.

The alcohol sickness was on him, too, making lights spin before his eyes. He forced himself to breath regularly, looking down, trying to regulate his pulse by force of will. Then his natural strength rose up in his body and cleared his brain and his heart began to pound steadily. He commenced the upward climb.

CHAPTER EIGHT

THE STRAIGHT-EDGED backs of three buildings rose beside the alley. All the nonsense of decoration and false front was stripped from them. Seen from the rear, they showed the builder's mind as it really was. Down below, as Gloster climbed, the light in the alley shrunk smaller and smaller and commenced to throw out separate rays, unwearingly. Three other fire escapes jagged up the backs of the neighboring buildings, dodged the windows, climbed and climbed to the roofs. Behind one window whose shade was pulled down, a light burned and made a blind, yellow eye which had some sort of spiritual significance to Gloster. He could not tell what it meant but he knew that it filled him with fear.

Then he got to the window of Raskoi's room. He recognized it by the rank, sour breath of wine that issued. He climbed in over the sill. It was not wine alone that fogged the air. He felt that he had come into the lair of something less than man and more than beast.

He sat down on the arm of an overstuffed chair and waited for his heart to quiet again after the climb. He could hear Raskoi breathing in heavy sleep.

Gradually the light came into the room, not the light of moon or stars but the glow of the city reflected from the miserably low clouds. By degrees his eyes felt their way around the chairs, the table, the lump of darkness on the floor that was Raskoi.

The coat would be in a bedroom closet. He got back into the next room, softly. The bed was a square of pale gray. He leaned close to it and heard the girl breathing. She had not taken her chance to leave the big drunken beast. She would wait for the morning, and money. If Raskoi gave her enough money no doubt she would stay on and hate him and serve him. Perhaps he would beat her into some sort of an affection, if he cared to take the time.

She began to whisper in her sleep: *"Je ne sais pas. Je ne sais pas. . . ."*

Gloster stepped back from the bed. He tried the wall to his right, running his hand up and down for doorknobs. When he found one, it was cold glass, cut to crisp edges. He opened the door. On the inside wall his hand touched the icy tiles of a bathroom.

He went on exploring. The next door opened on a closet filled with shelves. Another door gave him access, at last, to a coat closet. He touched the rough flimsy of a woman's coat, then a man's jacket. That must be Raskoi's.

He stepped inside the closet, closed the door until it was only an inch ajar, and used the little flat pocket torch which he carried. The shaft of light made a spot of burning white on the wall, with yellowed circles around the central core. He could see everything very well.

He went through the pockets of the jacket. He found an old-fashioned turnip watch with a heavy case of soft gold, dented in several places. It ticked too loudly to suit Gloster but it was telling the correct time. A gold chain connected with the watch, and at the end of the chain there was a big green, rough stone, an uncut emerald. A flat round of steel projected under the left armpit of the coat. He pulled at it and a straight-bladed dagger came out. He fitted the thing into his hand and the double-edged blade projected between his second and third fingers. He pushed the knife back into the leather scabbard which was sewn inside the lining of the coat. He found a cigarette lighter of English make, a cheap comb with some of the fine teeth broken out and hair twisted in among them, speckled with dandruff. There was a notebook, one side of it stiffened with cardboard to make it firm for writing upon.

He opened the book and commenced to run through the pages. The Russian was hard for him to read but he made it out. The opening insert was:

Merciful God, lead by the hand, guide with your voice your pitiful servant, Gregor Raskoi, who lies here weeping at your feet.

On another page:

Under the fingernails! What a fool I was to forget to connect the current under the fingernails. It must be like driving splinters into the quick. How much time I waste, being a fool!

Again:

Up, Raskoi! Up, up, Raskoi! Up, up! . . .
Well he makes me his dog, but I will bite all the other dogs. I will drive them mad. I will make them foam at the mouth. Mad dog! Mad dog! . . .

Oh woman when shall I find a mate? Why do you

crumble under my hands? Why do you melt away in my arms? Why are you softer than butter! Beasts, you are not worth buying, you are not worth having as a gift. On a black day, God threw you down on earth. He swept you out of heaven. He saw you fall. Afterward, he began to ache all over but he was free of you.

Several pages followed filled with figures very neatly written in and totaled. Perhaps these were expense accounts. Then:

She was fat all over, like a swine, and she squealed like a swine. She never had to draw breath after the current struck her under the fingernails. She never stopped screeching. Wonderful, wonderful lungs! . . .

Miserable Gregor, lowest of beasts. God, behold him! . . .

Almost on the last written page he found, written in German, not in Russian:

Tuesday, 9:00 A.M., Adlon, Winterberg.

This was Monday. On Tuesday at nine in the morning a person named Winterberg was to be met, it seemed. Or was Raskoi to go from the Adlon to a place called Winterberg?

Here the door of the closet blew softly open. The lights of the bedroom snapped on and he saw Raskoi naked to the waist with his lips grinned back so that the stiff rolls of flesh bulged up under his eyes.

He did not speak, but reached a hand for Gloster's throat, and Gloster smashed a fist into the middle of that grin.

The blow jerked back Raskoi's head. Gloster came out of the closet behind a shower of blows. Blood spurted on the

74

face of Raskoi but his head was India rubber. It was knocked back and forth and yet his body swayed back only a small step with each shock. The girl sat up in her bed with a screaming face but it seemed to Gloster that she made no sound. He was cutting his hands against the teeth of Raskoi and against the hard, bony ridges of his brows and jaw.

The Russian ducked in under a driving punch. He caught Gloster around the body and buried his teeth in the coat and shoulder. The pain was fire, as though Raskoi were biting out a lump of flesh; and all the while he kept kicking up with one knee. There was no end to the strength of his arms. They tightened and tightened like rope cable. They crushed the wind out of Gloster's lungs so that he began to bite at the air like a dog which is held by the throat. He had his right hand free and with the second knuckles he began to beat behind the ear of Raskoi. The flesh turned white. It split. The blood ran down.

Suddenly Raskoi winced and jumped back into the living room doorway. Gloster could not follow. His heart, thundering in his throat, choked him. Then, behind Raskoi, he saw a dim ghost with a maniac's face. A bottle swayed up in two hands and came down on the head of Raskoi. The glass did not break but the bone crunched. Raskoi dropped on his face.

He had not made a sound. Neither had the woman as she struck. There was only the fat, plopping noise as the loose flesh of Raskoi struck the floor. Blood was running into the matted hair at the back of his head.

"Look at him," said the girl through her teeth. "Is he dead?"

Gloster looked at the smashed head. "He's dead," he answered.

"He's dead—the beast!" nodded the girl.

"There's blood on your face," said Gloster. "Go wash it

off. And then dress."

She got as far as the bed and fell on it, her arms twined around her head. Gloster went into the next room and lighted a cigarette in the darkness. The burning coal drew out to a long, crooked, red triangle; the heat of the smoke scalded his tongue.

He turned on the lights and opened a bottle of Burgundy. At the first swallow, his heart stopped racing and his stomach was warmly comforted. It was good Burgundy. There was nothing green in its taste. It was a little sweet but all Burgundy is a little sweet. It was full of marrow and fruit, as the Frenchmen say. He found himself thinking about the wine and nothing else in spite of the other things that needed thought. The night voice of the city groaned in the streets and the memory of Lady Cecil came up to him, embodied in the sound.

Gradually a door opened in his mind. He kept slamming the door shut, turning away from the grim opportunity which lay ahead, but still with a quiet logic the thought persisted.

Russia was far away and Russian leaders were not publicized in the western world. Their faces were little known. People knew how Stalin looked, and that's about all.

He went back into the bedroom. "Get up and dress," he said to the girl.

She did not move.

He turned the body of Raskoi on its back and looked at the face for a long moment. Then he studied himself in the mirror. There were disheartening differences. Fear began to come up in him as when a man drives an automobile too fast and frightens himself and still keeps on driving faster and faster. He knew that he would follow out the idea which had entered his brain. At last he surrendered to it entirely and began to act upon it.

76

He pulled the trousers off Raskoi. There was a spot of blood on the knee of one trouser leg. He undressed. Raskoi's trousers were a little too big around the waist and hips but they were not a very bad fit. In the closet he found Raskoi's gray flannel shirt. There was a black necktie to go with it. In a suitcase were more shirts, underwear, socks of soft wool, some Russian cigarettes, a flask of vodka, a volume of Pushkin, a pack of goosequill toothpicks, two packs of cards, a big automatic, loaded, and an automobile map of Germany.

He took a swallow of the vodka; it seemed to send smoke out through his nostrils but it was good vodka.

Yes, there was heart in it.

He took off the trousers again and dressed himself from underwear out, completely, in the clothes of Raskoi. In the shoulders the coat pinched him a trifle; in the waist everything was still a bit too large, but on the whole he was comfortably dressed. There were stains on the front of the coat, which was a good, tough tweed, of dark gray. One of the stains was grease; another was sticky, perhaps from a sweet of some sort, and the dark red Burgundy had left its traces, naturally. Gloster seemed to see it hanging in drops from the chin of the Russian.

He had hard work, then, dragging his own clothes onto the body of Raskoi. When that was done, he picked up the hulk under the arms and dragged it to the coat closet. He took out the girl's coat and Raskoi's old raincoat, which was black with grease around the inside of the collar. Then he shoveled the body of Raskoi into the closet, locked the door, and dropped the key into his pocket.

After that, he washed in the bathroom. His hands had stopped bleeding. He pulled off some bits of loose skin from his knuckles and then noticed that the hands were swelling a little. Back in the bedroom he leaned over the girl.

77

"Get up!" he commanded.

She lay as though senseless. He turned her on her back and made her sit up. Her eyes were dead, her face twisted into set lines of nausea.

"You've got to dress," said Gloster. "Try this. It will buck you up."

Her head went back helplessly against his shoulder and he poured a long swallow of the vodka down her throat. That got her off the bed and made her stand up, shuddering.

"Listen to me," said Gloster. "He's dead. Raskoi! Raskoi is dead!"

"I killed him," she whispered. She looked up at him with the smile of a contented child. "I killed him!" she said, and closed her eyes again.

He wrapped her in a blanket, and laid her on the bed, because the coldness of her body alarmed him.

"Who sent you to pick up Raskoi?" he asked. She lay with her eyes closed and made no answer. "Raskoi! Why did you kill him?" asked Gloster. "Raskoi—you hear me?"

"Winton Jones," she whispered. "Am I going to die?"

"You've had a shock, but you're not going to die," said Gloster. "You're getting better fast. In ten minutes you'll be all right."

"I want to sleep! I'm sleepy, Monsieur Gloster. . . ."

The name had hit him hard. He wanted to have Winton Jones there and curse him. The color was coming back in her face, now. "Did Winton Jones tell you to kill Raskoi?" he asked.

She opened her sleeping eyes suddenly and said: "God told me to! I saw my brother screaming and dying and Raskoi laughing. I saw . . ."

She sat up in bed. Her voice went into a screech. Gloster put his hand over her mouth. The softness of the lips kept

78

struggling against the palm of his hand. After a moment she fell back into the pillows and lay there, panting.

A hand tapped on the living room door.

"Will you be quiet?" asked Gloster. She looked up at him with frightened eyes and nodded, so he went into the living room, singing loudly the old Volga song which goes something like this:

> My sweetheart wears but wooden shoes
> Wooden shoes, wooden shoes;
> And a sack around her middle,
> A sack around her middle,
> And a skewer through her hair!

He roughed up his hair, took a bottle in his hand, and opened the door. A big man with a hard, square, Prussian face stood in the hall.

"The noise, Herr Raskoi!" he said. "The trampling and dancing and the singing. How can your neighbors sleep?"

"Pour this down their throats," said Gloster. "That will choke off their complaints. And what's left pour down your own throat and choke yourself, and be damned!"

He thrust the bottle of Burgundy into the hands of the clerk and shut the door in his face. The hand did not tap on his door again. He waited, feeling a greater and a greater strength. A voice inside him seemed to be speaking.

He lighted a cigarette and went into the bedroom. He was amazed to see the girl already dressed, sitting in front of the mirror to do her hair. She smiled over her shoulder at Gloster, lifting her eyebrows in a question.

"All right," said Gloster.

He watched her face and throat in the mirror. It was a street dress but it had a collar of fluffy lace that framed the picture softly. She was no longer beneath desire. She seemed to know the difference when she stood up and met his eye. She straightened the dress with her hands and put on a pale blue hat that slouched to one side and had a red feather in it.

"Now that I'm all ready, do you really want me to go?" she asked.

"Do you know what's in there?" asked Gloster.

She looked toward the coat closet without the slightest shock or disgust.

"I wonder what part of hell he's in?" she asked.

"Come along," said Gloster. "You're getting out of here."

"Yes, Monsieur Gloster."

"Raskoi," said Gloster.

She looked at his clothes and nodded, as she started for the door. "But that won't do," she said, pointing to the floor.

On the painted wood the blood of Raskoi lay in streaks and globules, like red oil. She went into the bathroom, brought out a wet washrag and cleaned the floor. Afterward, she rinsed the rag clean, scrupulously clean, in the wash-bowl, and dropped it over the edge of the bathtub. When she came out she said:

"He didn't tie his necktie like that. Have you forgotten? This way."

She undid the tie and unbuttoned the neck of the shirt.

"It was open like this," she said, "and he made two wrappings—so—Monsieur Raskoi. *Comme ça.*"

She smiled at him as she worked.

"Are you all right?" asked Gloster. "You *look* all right."

She nodded. "I'm happy. I could sing," she said. "I could sing—and dance on his dead face! Are you sure you want me to go?"

"Yes," said Gloster. "How much money have you?"

"Plenty. I don't need money," she told him.

He took her purse and counted eight hundred Reichsmarks

in it. "That's not enough," he said, and gave her two thousand more.

She merely said, "It's not right. I ought to do the paying! I've had the pleasure."

"Now come along," said Gloster, and took her from the rooms into the hall.

He was rumbling deep in his throat, as they took the elevator down, the same old Volga boat song:

> My sweetheart has but wooden shoes,
> Wooden shoes, wooden shoes. . . .

They walked out onto the main floor, where rugs were rolled up and the cleaners scrubbed busily. They scrubbed on their hands and knees, working thoroughly. No one was was visible behind the semicircle of the desk and he was glad of that. They walked out into Unter den Linden and saw the dreary gray of the morning beginning on the horizon, making the sweep of windy clouds blacker and heavier. A taxi driver saluted like a soldier. Gloster waved him away and they walked on through the great Brandenburger Tor with its silly horses galloping endlessly into the sky above them.

"Where do you go?" he asked.

"Zum Westen," she said.

"Get out of Berlin," said Gloster. "I'm going to leave you now. Get out of Berlin. Get out of Germany. You'd better take a plane and fly out. Go fast. The German police are the devil."

She dropped a hand on her hip and surveyed him with a smiling deliberation.

"Do you think I'm afraid to die?" she asked. Her head jerked back with a full, free burst of laughter. "Do you think I'm afraid to die?" she repeated.

81

Chapter Nine

He went back to the hotel, and took an elevator with two couples who had been out doing the town. When he got out at his floor he heard the elevator boy saying through the closing doors, "Raskoi . . ."

And one of the women almost screamed, "What? Raskoi? . . ."

The closing of the metal doors shut out the voices; only the whirring of the elevator was audible as he went down the hall, wondering if he had played the part well enough. But after all even Raskoi must have his down moments and could not be continually exploding. He put his hand on the knob of the door and waited there for a long moment before he pushed it open. But nothing lived in the room except the blue stallion galloping over the green hill into the sky.

He looked into the bedroom. A blanket had fallen to the floor; the top sheet was twisted into strings and wrinkles. On the floor he examined the bare paint and then the rug but found no recent stains. He had had a sense that blood was flowing and spattering from the beginning of the fight and yet the only blood had been on the spot where Raskoi fell.

The living room looked like a stable, with the broken bottle necks and the littered straw jackets in which the Burgundy was packed. He lay down on the couch, folded his hands on his stomach, and closed his eyes. Weariness set an ache behind them; alcohol weighted the base of his brain. And then sleep in great numb waves seemed to move upwards from his feet. It broke in showers of darkness across his mind.

At eight o'clock a tap on the door half roused him; a mechanic stole in with a kit of tools. Gloster cursed him in Russian, then in German. The blond Prussian reddened with savage anger and set his teeth and went on working at the broken telephone. Gloster closed his eyes and snored, with a deep, rattling intake and a whistle with each outward breath.

"Swine!" said the mechanic under his breath. *"Schwein!"* he whispered again, as he left the room.

Gloster sat up and used the telephone. "Breakfast!" he shouted. "No damned German *Frühstück, hören Sie?* This is Raskoi! You hear me? Caviar, and half a dozen boiled eggs, and some fat pork. Fat, you hear? And a quart of black coffee; and some stale bread. Stale bread, I tell you, sheep's head, wooden block!"

Breakfast came and two frightened waiters with it. Gloster snored on the couch till they were gone. Then he ate what he could and threw the rest away.

At nine o'clock, precisely, came the rap on his door.

"Herein!" shouted Gloster.

The door opened on a tall man with a long, thin face and hair dead white above the ears, dead black over the rest of the head.

"Winterberg?" asked Gloster, without rising.

"Winterberg?" exclaimed the German. "No, Herr Raskoi.

Hans Graustein, only—to serve you, Herr Raskoi, if you will come with me?"

"Where?" said Gloster, rubbing his eyes and yawning.

"Where they agreed to wait, Herr Raskoi," said Graustein, looking puzzled.

"My face itches," said Gloster. "I'll shave first."

"But, Herr Raskoi, they all are waiting! They are ready!" said Graustein.

"Let them wait and be damned for it," said Gloster. "I told you my face itches."

He went into the bathroom and shaved, deliberately, and as he shaved he sang, over and over, the chorus of a Moscow street ballad, full of Oriental whine and with very little tune at all.

Graustein was a very nervous man when Gloster went down with him to the street to a closed automobile that whipped them out through Friedrichstrasse and stopped in front of an old stone house with a brown front and a coat of arms over the door, a unicorn and a bear rampant on either side of a disk covered with indistinguishable figures.

The door opened into a big hall with a double staircase rising from the farther end of it, and a huge, crystal chandelier descended from the middle of the ceiling. It was more of a palace than a home.

Graustein took Gloster through two or three rooms with gilded consoles in the corners and many great mirrors and rugs that flamed hotter than fire underfoot. Finally, opening a door, Graustein bowed him into a library done in time-darkened oak, with racks of books rising eight feet all around the room, and hunting trophies affixed to the walls above.

"Herr Raskoi!" announced Graustein, and four men rose in the room to greet him.

One of them came forward. He had a face like a wolf,

heavy in the jaws, meager in the muzzle, with wise wrinkles of thought cleaving the middle of his forehead. His manner was distinguished, calm, and easy. He took Gloster by the hand.

"Von Emsdorf," he said. "A great pleasure, Gregor Raskoi."

He brought Gloster on toward the fireplace where five-foot logs were hissing and burning without throwing up a clear flame.

"Conte di Parva—Herr Johann Gleich—Monsieur Jacques Louvain," said von Emsdorf.

Gloster noted them one by one. The Belgian, Louvain, was a fat man who was so short of wind that he panted as he smoked his cigar, holding it exactly in the middle of his mouth and making almost inaudible smacking noises with his lips. He was sixty, at least.

The Austrian, Johann Gleich, was only a lad of twenty-eight. He looked like an athlete and a desperado and sneered every moment as though he found what each moment contained really beneath any serious interest.

Conte di Parva represented the hearty contadino type of Italian, with plenty of neck girth and not much back to his head; and yet there was something about his big face, the very crook and size of his huge nose, that assured Gloster that the man was of a very old family, indeed.

They greeted Raskoi one after the other, and Johann Gleich said: "We've been waiting almost an hour for you, Herr Raskoi."

"I would have made you wait two, but I felt good-natured this morning," said Raskoi.

The four looked at him silently. Young Johann Gleich ran the red tip of his tongue over his lips.

"You little Westerners," said Gloster, "have to get used to waiting for the real people." He turned his back on them and spat into the fire. "Give me some Burgundy," said Gloster. "I'll be on time to drink that, anyway!" And he put back his head and roared with laughter.

They kept on looking at him, silently. Then von Emsdorf walked to the wall and pressed a bell.

"Little Westerners! said Gloster, waving his hand. "Little people with no backyards. You have to plant your crops in your cellars. Get away from me! I laugh! Raskoi, he laughs! . . . I kept you waiting? You thank God that I came at all and don't start talk about waiting."

"I'm going to tell you," said the hard, ringing voice of Johann Gleich, "that your Russian . . ."

Gleich looked down at his hand, made it into a fist, and then slowly relaxed the fingers one by one. When he looked up, he had himself under control again.

Good-natured Jacques Louvain said, "You know, Gregor Raskoi, it seems to me that you've grown a new face since I last saw you in Russia."

Von Emsdorf was prodding at the fire with a long poker. He turned his wolf's head, slowly, and looked Gloster in the eye.

"Yes, I have a new face," said Gloster. "And it cost me money to get it. You know how I got it?" He laughed and went on without waiting for the question. "Burgundy! You water your wheat with red wine and it will be red wheat! I used to be thin. When you saw me, little man, I used to be light. But now when I come they hear my step on the stairs. Yes, they hear me on the stairs and it makes their flesh crawl. They hear my footstep and they hear my voice, too. Because I come singing. In Russia there's no room for filthy aristocrats; there's no room for counts or viscounts, either, and there's no room for fat bankers, but there's room for a man and his song, too. You hear that, all of you?"

No one answered him. A servant came to the door.

"Herr Raskoi will have some Burgundy. Red Burgundy,"

said von Emsdorf. "What sort will you like, Herr Raskoi?"

"What sort will I like? What is the best? The best may be good enough for me. Bring me a bottle of Romanée Conti."

The cold, even voice of von Emsdorf said, "A bottle of Romanée Conti. I think there is a little left."

But the German had flushed, and the big muscles at the base of his jaw were bulging.

"You know," said Louvain, "it still is rather strange to me. I wouldn't have recognized Gregor Raskoi. And yet I sat at the same table with him. The table was rather long, to be sure. I thought it was quite a different face."

"Ah, did you?" asked von Emsdorf.

"I did," said Louvain, with increased surety.

Von Emsdorf drew some papers from his pocket and selected an envelope from among them.

"Have you any specimens of your handwriting, Herr Raskoi?" he asked.

"Specimens? Why should I show you specimens? I show specimens to doctors, not to von Emsdorfs. But if you want to see if Gregor Raskoi can write, he can! Look for yourself!"

He snatched out the notebook of Raskoi and flung it at von Emsdorf. The German caught it in his hand, stared a cold moment at Gloster, and then opened the little book.

He read aloud:

> For roasted pig's head, plenty of mustard, roast apples, soft bread for the gravy, served by a maiden if you can find one in Russia.

Gloster shouted with laughter. He took hold of the back of a chair and laughed some more.

Von Emsdorf closed the notebook, flicked the pages with the edge of his thumb, and returned it to Gloster with a bow.

"You write very well, Gregor Raskoi," he said. "You write—with great deal of feeling."

"I write what's in me," said Gloster, "and by God, some of it would take the skin off your noses. Some of it is hot enough to burn."

"Do you bring me any word from our friend of the Central Executive Committee?" asked von Emsdorf.

"Ah, ha," said Gloster. "I know what you mean. Our Beloved and Bold, our Wise Inspirer, our Genius, our Shockworker, our Best of the Best, our Guiding Star, our Comrade, our Friend, our Stalin! That's the one you mean, is it?"

"That is the one I mean," said von Emsdorf.

"I carry my master's words in my brain, not in my pocket," said Gloster. "I'm the dog that barks when he bids me but I put my teeth in other men."

"Yes," said Louvain, suddenly. "That's Gregor Raskoi. That sounds like him."

"But if you want to know what authority sends me here," said Gloster, "I'll tell you. It's the authority of Gregor Raskoi. Is that good enough for you? You, Gleich, or whatever your damned name is, is that good enough for you? Do you want something more? Don't rouse me, you little Westerners. Look at my hands! I barked the skin off them on a woman's head but there's plenty of tough wood under the bark, and I can use it on weak-hearted, puling, soft-faced, white-bellied aristocrats! You—I mean you, Gleich!"

"Johann!" barked von Emsdorf.

Johann Gleich turned his back and walked to a window with his head bowed.

Von Emsdorf said, "If you keep on talking like this, Johann Gleich will murder you, Gregor Raskoi."

"Ah, will he?" asnewered Gloster. "Will he do that? Perhaps I was wrong. Perhaps he is my brother. Gleich, come and give me your hand."

Gleich turned slowly, with a white face.

"Johann, give him your hand," said von Emsdorf.

Johann Gleich crossed the room and touched the hand of Gloster silently. Behind him, von Emsdorf's German shepherd dog slunk suddenly out of a corner where it had lain as obscure as the shadows, and as though it recognized with a devilish surety the passion that was in the young Austrian. It now slipped along at his heels, and shrank away again as he turned and left Gloster.

Gleich merely said as he took the hand of Gloster. "I won't save your words like money!"

Then von Emsdorf took control of the group and pushed forward their business.

"We have not much time," he said. "The fewer moments we spend together the better, as you all will agree. And there is nothing in our work that cannot be done suddenly. Raskoi, here is your wine. Take this chair. Parva, let's hear from you, first."

"I cannot tell you exactly how Italy will move. If anybody could read the mind of Il Duce," said Parva, "he would be leader himself and Mussolini would be something else. But I think he will act if he has the chance; that is to say, if there is some opportunity which opens the door. Our last normal year was 1934. The deficit that year was half a billion dollars.

"Do any of you realize what half a billion dollars a year means in a poor country like Italy? Il Duce can't afford to let the country stand still and discover what's happening to it. Forty percent of the total income of the country goes into the national revenue. Can any of you imagine that? And in addition, there's the five percent capital levy collected! More than a year's income at a stroke.

"If Il Duce allows the country to pause, it may be overwhelmed wtih despair. It has to go forward. Where? It's hard to tell. Take a slice out of Yugoslavia? Those Yugoslavs are hard fighters, and they offer us nothing but barren mountains and highlands. Rumania, Turkey, and Greece are solidly behind them. That's why we turn north and look at France because of her colonies. Show us a gate that can be opened and we'll move. Not because we hate France but because we can't stand and starve outside the only door that can be opened."

"This is more than mere thinking? You've made wide inquiries, Count?" asked von Emsdorf.

"Among the people of whom I told you. No, it is not mere thinking."

"Now you, Louvain?" asked von Emsdorf.

The fat man's cigar waved.

"There is a party in my country, as you know," said Louvain, with his pleasant smile, "which never wanted to be tied to France and the gold bloc. It has seen the gold bloc fall and it is ready for change. The party is quiet, but it is very strong. If a powerful movement were made toward France south of Belgium, I can guarantee that there would be no flank attack delivered by the Belgian army on the invaders. It would remain on the frontier to observe. It would stay there observing."

"In spite of the treaties?" said von Emsdorf.

Louvain laughed a little. "Treaties? Today?" he murmured. "My dear von Emsdorf! After Ethiopia? After the occupation of the Rhineland?"

Everyone in the room smiled, except Johann Gleich.

"We would see to it—we peace-lovers—that there would be no Belgian flank attack," said Louvain.

"And you, Gleich?" asked von Emsdorf.

Gleich said in his clear, rapid voice, "It is better to starve in company than to starve alone. Austria would join Germany for a strong blow; and Austria would be linked to Germany forever. Blood tells. We are the same blood."

"And Russia?" said von Emsdorf.

Gloster lifted the bottle and poured a long draft down his throat. He lowered the bottle. A few drops ran down on his chin and collected there.

"Latvia—Estonia—Lithuania—" he said, and felt the drop fall from his chin and gave no heed.

He saw the face of Gleich twist with disgust and straighten gradually again.

"Go on, please," urged von Emsdorf.

"Go on!" said Gloster, waving his right hand. "Go on West, you little peoples. We will take the East. And if Poland jumps on your back when you turn West—Russia will take a slice of Polish cheese. We have good stomachs. We digest bad meat easily!" He laughed as he said it.

"Stalin?" asked von Emsdorf.

"Yes, Stalin," said Gloster, nodding, and half closing his eyes.

"He understands what we must have. We need Germany, because Germany is full of machines which we must have. Germany can make them. We will buy them, little machinists. Yes, yes, we will buy many of them. You will be able to drink your beer and get fat again and smoke your crooked pipes and beat your wives—"

He laughed, leaning back in his chair, thrusting his legs straight out. In this moment, von Emsdorf looked steadily at and observed the big shepherd dog, black as night and yellow-eyed, come stealthily up to the hand of Gloster; and the hand of Gloster, absently, as though of its own volition, found the head of the dog and stroked it, found the shoulder of the big beast, drew it close to his chair, and went on caressing, with an instinctive, wandering gentleness of touch. The eyes of von Emsdorf narrowed as he watched.

"So——" he said. "It is enough! We meet again this evening, here. Then I will show you what gate is to be opened."

"Do you mean that we stop now, when we've hardly commenced?" snapped Gleich.

Von Emsdorf let his glance rest upon each of the faces around. His eye was bright, his voice a silken rustle:

"We've more than commenced. We've seen the faces of one another. We've heard one another speak. This evening I'm going to start opening the Western door for you. I shall show you the way."

Von Emsdorf sat at the table alone when the others had gone from the room. Heavy doors hushed away all sounds from this inner place, yet the echoes of Gloster's great laughter still remained with him. There was black earth in that laughter, the German thought, and it was unclean.

His long finger felt along the sagging line of his jowl. . . . Louvain—yes, that fat one could be counted on. Slow, perhaps—a coward surely—yet Louvain was an old hand who knew the traitor's penalty too well. . . . Di Parva—a parrot only. A puppet who spoke the words he had been taught. . . . Johann Gleich, a patriot, a firebrand. Yes, that was the surest kind. . . .

But Raskoi—? What of Gregor Raskoi?

Von Emsdorf's lean lips compressed. His narrowed eyes pondered infinitely. They had warned him, of course, that the Russian was half-devil, half-cur. Trouble walked in the footsteps of Raskoi. Why had they sent such a filthy pig with so much weighed in the balance?

He leaned back his head and his fingertips touched. Little mechanics, eh? The Romanée Conti only he would drink? He would treat them like the unwashed dogs—?

"Ah," said von Emsdorf softly. *"Dogs. . . ."*

Yes, it might be that they had sent this Raskoi to defile and insult them all. To make a furor of this meeting and dynamite all plans. Yet Stalin was too wise for that. There was too much to be gained.

"Dogs—" he said again, and his thin lips pursed.

He turned in his chair and his gaze was bright upon the black shepherd that was stretched out near the fireplace.

Chapter Ten

THE BEER garden band broke into the wailing lechery of *Tristan* as Cailland was saying: ". . . in every corridor, imagine, guards; and in the open yards that surrounded the building, more guards, and an outer wall fifteen feet high, constantly watched. You would say: 'How possibly could a man enter the place?' "

"It makes me shudder a little, Jules," said Lady Cecil, "but at the same time I love it. I can't imagine how you got in, unless you were a mole and burrowed, or put on wings and dropped out of the air."

"Can't you imagine, Cecil?" asked Cailland, smiling a little. "But tell me, now. You don't dislike this place, and the beer?"

"I adore it."

"There aren't so many bright days in Berlin," said Cailland, "and when there's a sun to warm one—and the trees are such a luminous yellow-green—"

"But I love it, Jules. Only, go on with the story."

"Ah, but it isn't a story," he said.

"No I know that."

"Another litre, Cecil?"

94

"No. A demi. I couldn't take another glass. There isn't room. But the story—please, Jules!"

"Well, the answer was simply that there was no way to steal into the building."

"But you got there?"

"By walking in."

"Good heavens, Jules! No!"

"You know, my dear, the divine thing in a spy is patience. Ah, I'm a mundane fellow but I do have a little patience. So first I found out the names and the addresses of the five men who were working on the drawings for the great gun. You've no idea, perhaps, how complicated the drawings for a great gun may be! Almost like designs for a battleship. So many problems of recoil, and all that, have to be dealt with, you see."

"Of course," said the girl.

"My problem was to get the drawings, so first I ran all the five draftsmen to earth. One was a little old man with a sweet pair of blue eyes and one was a fellow with only one leg, a war veteran, and another was hardy Scot from the Clyde, and there was a fat little chunk of a man who wore great glasses; but the fifth man was within an inch of my height. If he had not glaring red hair, which curled all over his head, he would have looked just a little like me, except that he had great lines incised by his nose."

"Jules, do I begin to see?"

"Yes, there was the idea. I went to live in the same boarding house with him. We became friends. I studied his face. I became familiar with his room. You see, Cecil, if you expect to succeed in this work it's not a matter of arriving at a place, performing a brilliant miracle and then walking away again—one must take time and be patient."

"I know! I know!" said Lady Cecil. "It's living with danger, breathing it day and night."

"Well, at last the night came. I spent the entire afternoon in my room. Sick, I told the landlady. I curled my hair until it stood out an inch above my ears. I dyed it a violent red, and then I put on clothes exactly like the clothes of my friend the draftsman. There were the lines to work into my face, too, so I put in a pair of deep shadows, like cuts. And then I was ready, so I went down and picked the lock of my friend's door."

"Will you teach me how to do that, Jules?"

"Of course. In two or three years you can learn the trick, if you have a bit of aptitude."

"Good heavens—two or three years? But I shall be patient!"

"Then I went into the room and got his card and his keys from his clothes. After that, I went straight over to the place and offered the card to the officer in charge of the gate house. He was one of those Frenchmen with the wine-sour look, a sallow face, a mole on his cheek, and no smiles. He looked at my card and he looked at me when I told him that I had to push through some night work, by order. He called a watchman. The night watchman gave me one look and a yawn. 'He's all right,' he said. So I went on through. My card passed me by the inner guards and I went down the corridor to the proper room—I'd learned the location from my friend the draftsman. I opened the door and walked in—and there was the fat man with the glasses hard at work!"

"Ah, Jules, how frightful!"

"I didn't speak to him, because of course he would have noticed the strangeness of my voice. I had to trust that the thick lenses of his glasses would make me a figure in a mist. The number on my key told me the number of the locker where my friend's drawing materials were secured, so I went straight across the room to it. The fat man spoke to me and called me 'Luigi'—that was the name of my poor friend.

96

I couldn't answer. I merely made a gesture with both arms above my head, like a fellow too disgusted with life and hard times, and then I unlocked the cabinet and got out the material. Imagine, that I didn't even know how to set up the drawing board!"

"Jules! What was your heart doing?"

"Ah, well, one's heart must stay in the right place. Otherwise one should have nothing to do with such business. No, in every pinch I must count on my heart behaving. But there I was, killing time, setting up the board, and of course the moment I started work the fat fellow would know that I was a pretender if he glanced at what I was doing. I suppose his glasses prevented him from looking too closely at me; and I kept my hat slouched down on the side nearest to him. I put in time cleaning up the drawing with the eraser. At last he stood up and yawned, then put away his materials, waved his hand, and was gone like a shot. I blessed him for that. Then I started work. I had to open all the lockers, get out the drawings, fold them around my body, and dress again. But the thing ended, somehow, and before dawn I walked out with the whole secret of that great gun in my pocket. So I went back to the boarding house—"

"No! What if you had been seen?"

"It was just a little too early for that. I went up to my room and fixed my hair and makeup; I slipped down into my friend's room and put the card and keys in his clothes."

"And then fled for your life?"

"Not at all! I didn't want to have them on my trail. I waited for two days before I left the boarding house, and said a very affectionate farewell to my friend the red-head. . . ."

"Ah Monsieur Jacquelin!" whispered the girl.

"Hush!" he cautioned her, lifting a finger.

"I couldn't help it," she answered. "And tell me the truth.

You were not telling me how you got the plans of a great gun, merely. You were telling me how you secured the plans of the Maginot Line!"

"Cecil, you will not be made a detective. You were born one," admitted Cailland.

She said, "It seems to me, Jules, that I'd rather sit with Monsieur Jacquelin—I swear I won't use the name again today—than with one of the bright angels . . . on a golden throne, and all."

"Cecil, do you know that you torture me?" said Cailland.

"I? I?" cried the girl.

"Sometimes when I see your eyes and sometimes when I hear you, it seems to me almost like love, and my heart comes rushing out to welcome it, and then you withdraw, as you would withdraw now, if I said that I loved you, Cecil. If I said that I adored you, and begged you to marry me!"

"Would I withdraw?" she asked, looking up past him, at her own thought.

He rested his big chin on his fist and stared at her, hopelessly.

"It isn't I that you care about," he said. "It's only things that I have done. My God, Cecil, it seems hard, doesn't it? I mean, that a man's past should be separated from him, and not a part of himself?"

"I do love what you've done," said the girl.

"But not Jules Cailland?"

"I hardly know you at all."

"If I could wipe out of your mind," said Cailland, "the memory of some one man, how would it be with you then, Cecil?"

"I suppose there would be nothing but Jules left," she admitted.

"Will you tell me about him?"

"Why, he's a funny, rough fellow," she said. "And he has

a crazy dash and go to him. I think I would have married him before this except that I've fallen in love with this new life, Jules. And when I look at him and his foolish, head-long impulsiveness I realize how far he is from being a Monsieur Jacquelin. It's as though he were everything I wanted except that he lacks that special leavening. Does that seem foolish, Jules?"

"No. Tell me, do I know him?"

"Yes."

"It's Gloster!" exclaimed Cailland.

"Yes. It's Willie. What does he think of me now, Jules, when he realizes that I've gone off into a strange country with a man I'd never seen before? What does he think?"

She covered her face with her hands for an instant, and then forced herself to brighten.

"But that's a price I have to pay," she said. "Don't I, Jules? It's only the beginning of frightful things that people will think about me, but some day I'll begin to have my reward. Perhaps now—in Berlin—perhaps we shall have a chance to match wits with them, and fight in secret, and go through some great and appalling and glorious moment of danger . . . do you think, Jules, that there is a ghost of a chance?"

"I think there is. A ghost," said Cailland. "There's von Emsdorf. No use bringing him here. He wouldn't talk at our table, and I don't want him to see your face. Keep your head down a little. I'll go talk to him!"

He got up in haste and greeted the tall German at a little distance from the table.

"We'll take another place," he said. "We can't talk in front of other people, obviously.

"Do you know that girl at your table?" asked von Emsdorf.

"Oh, well enough," said Cailland.

"What is she?" asked the German.

"English, and a fool," said Cailland.

"And what else?" asked von Emsdorf. "Lost her head about you? I recognize her, my dear Cailland. She is in the English service."

"She's a pretty thing, eh, and she's no great bother," said Cailland. "She won't be in my way. Shall I tell you her reason for being in Berlin? Come closer. She is hunting for the plans of the Maginot Line! The same ones you relieved her of in London!"

"She's hunting for *me,* then?" asked von Emsdorf, smiling.

"Exactly," said Cailland.

"She looks like a pretty dish," said von Emsdorf. "She might be useful to me this afternoon. Bring her around to my house for cocktails at five."

"Certainly," said Cailland.

"Jacquelin . . ." said von Emsdorf.

The head of Cailland rose a little. "What about him?" he asked.

The wolfish face of von Emsdorf had sharpened a little. "Cailland," he said, "either you actually were with Jacquelin, or else you are Jacquelin himself. I've checked back every one of the statements you made in *La Liberté* and they seem to be true."

"I was hand in glove with him for a time," said Cailland.

"Jacquelin never associated himself with anybody," answered von Emsdorf. "Cailland, you are Monsieur Jacquelin!"

Cailland drew a breath that raised his shoulders in a shrug. "My dear fellow," he said, "if you have a conviction, why should I argue with you—particularly in a beer garden?"

"I want you," said von Emsdorf. "I need your brain.

100

Europe needs your brain," he added significantly.

"It's like a haunted house," said Cailland, smiling. "It's generally for rent. Which seems to bring us to money, doesn't it?"

"It does," agreed von Emsdorf.

"It seems to me," said Cailland, "that I deserve at least a half payment for getting the Maginot plans. My part of the contract was executed. I delivered the plans to the messenger. He actually got them into Germany. If he lost them there, is it really my fault?"

"Remember," said von Emsdorf, "that I did not lay eyes on them in Germany."

"They were set adrift, however," answered Cailland, "and that was why you were able to put your hands on them in London. Isn't that true?"

Von Emsdorf regarded space with a critical eye.

"A half payment," said Cailland, "would be seventy thousand dollars on my share."

The Prussian took a breath and made a sudden gesture. "It is yours!" he said.

"Von Emsdorf," said the Frenchman, "will you believe me when I say that you will be paying for more than the plans?"

"Shall I be buying a part in Monsieur Jacquelin?" murmured von Emsdorf.

"You shall," said Cailland.

"Good!" said von Emsdorf quietly. "Very good indeed. May I ask you one question first of all?"

"Yes. Certainly."

"You have been in Russia, I know. While you were there, did you ever lay eyes on the great beast, soldier, executioner, and drunkard, Raskoi?"

"I think I did. I think I would know him," answered Cailland.

"You will have a chance to see him this afternoon," said von Emsdorf. "How will you have that money, my friend?"

"In pounds sterling."

"The English still hold the trust of the world," said von Emsdorf bitterly. "A nation of tricksters and sharpers, but they still keep all the faith that the world can enclose in its pocketbook. There may be a change, Jacquelin. What cannot be taken with cash may be taken with the sword. Perhaps, Jacquelin, a road is opening before you wider than any you ever walked before!"

CHAPTER ELEVEN

THE BRIGHT warmth of the day lifted the heart of all Berlin, but it only spread a sleepy weariness through Gloster. He went back to the hotel and found there a note from von Emsdorf saying:

> Come at five if you can. I want you to have cocktails with some friends. I'll set you free again by six; and dinner will be at eight.

He put the note in his pocket and went to his room. In this state of mild drowsiness it was hard for him to remember that his part was that of the furiously volcanic Russian, Raskoi. When he came to the door of the room he found it ajar; a rattling noise was going on inside the apartment. It was the maid busily shaking the door of the coat closet.

"It's locked!" she exclaimed. "I can't imagine how . . ."

"Ha!" shouted Gloster. "But I can imagine that you are a thief! You are trying to get to my wine, are you? I'll pull the hair off your head like a wig, I'll—"

She ran from him with a screech and got away, leaving her broom and dustcloth behind her. Gloster threw them into the hall after her and lay down on the couch, but his thoughts kept walking back and forth between the living room and the closet where the body of Raskoi lay.

He had a sense that he was stopped and lashed to one place like a ship to a pier; but he had not much time, he had to be in motion. That sense of the need of action stifled him. His nerves jittered. So he lay back on the couch and sang to himself, softly, softly. He wanted the little accordion, but that lay in the coat pocket of the dead man in the coat closet.

At four forty-five he went to the house of von Emsdorf. The servants sent him down into the garden, for the great house was built around a court with three Palladian stories rising about it, and in the center of the court a little formal garden was arranged around a fountain. In the old days, there had been a carriage-way around the court paving stones, but the size of huge modern automobiles made the drive too cramped and so it had given way to grass which did the best it could in the damp, dark Berlin weather.

As he came down, he saw von Emsdorf under the arcade, and his heart leaped at the sight of Cailland and Lady Cecil beside the Prussian. Gloster waved a pint of Burgundy which he took out of his pocket.

"D'you see what I've done?" he shouted. "I've brought out the sun, and I've made it shine red, by God. I've brought out a Burgundy sun, and it's shining red on everything."

"Could the red be in your eye, Gregor Raskoi?" asked von Emsdorf. "I present to you Monsieur Jules Cailland."

"Ah, you are a Frenchman!" said Gloster. "There is one good thing about Frenchmen. They have gold for Russians to spend. They are little people but they have big purses and Russians know how to empty them. Give me gold, Monsieur Cailland. I will spend it for you. There is too much gold in France, but in Russia wherever a grain of the gold falls, a thousand acres of ground turn green and the wheat shoots up tender sprouts from the ground. Have you ever seen a tender shoot, Frenchman? Have you ever pushed from the ground and rejoiced in the first sun of spring? Have you ever heard the peasants singing in your honor? Monsieur Cailland, I drink to you! It is not Romanée Conti because that is a wine in which I cannot drink the health of a Frenchman; but in good Pommard I drink to you!"

"Talk to him," said von Emsdorf, privately. "Talk to him, Jacquelin. Test him. See if he is really Russian—really Raskoi!"

"What is your home place, Herr Raskoi?" asked Cailland.

"I come from *selo* Petrova," said Gloster. "Do you know where that is?"

"No. There are a thousand *selo* Petrovas in Russia," said Cailland.

"It is near *derievna* Nicolaevka," said Gloster.

"He lives," translated Cailland, "in Peterstown which has a church, which is near Nicholastown, that has no church at all. That is what he means. But there are ten thousand towns named after Peter, my friend, Gregor Raskoi."

"Are there?" said Gloster. "If you had a grain of Russian wit in your head you would know the place I mean, however."

"How far is it from Moscow?" asked Cailland.

"About three days and a half," said Gloster.

"Three days and a half of what?" said Cailland.

"Of travel by fast horses," said Gloster.

"In what direction?" asked Cailland.

"In the direction of the warmer winter," said Gloster. "Toward the early spring."

"He means toward the south," said Cailland. "How do people know your town when they come to it?"

"They know it from a long distance off," said Gloster. "By God, the five domes of our church shine like five suns and the crosses above the gilded domes are like five beautiful stars. Men are dazzled and women fall down and cry when they see *selo* Petrova."

"You are a good, religious fellow, I see," said Cailland.

"Religion? Religion can go to the devil," said Gloster. "Lenin was god enough for me. And after him, Stalin is enough of an angel. He can make this dog bark and he can make this dog bite. And that is more than any priest ever made me do. . . . Oh, Mother Russia, I drink to you. I wish to God that fine Burgundy would spring out of your soil like a fountain. Then I would never want to see any other land."

"Were you happy in your village before the revolution?" asked Cailland.

"Yes, happy enough. But my father told me that everybody was happier still in the days when everyone lived on the mir. After that fool Stolypin began to turn the peasants into farmers holding their own land, then there was grief. The priest went around with red eyes all the year, weeping for his people; and the *starosta* turned white in one year and died the next, trying to heal the hearts of the peasants. But in the good old days everybody grew fat together or everybody starved together and so one was as good as the other."

"Ah—ah," cautioned Cailland. "Does that sound like a good revolutionary?"

"When you are in Russia, go ask about me," said Gloster. "You will find the story written everywhere in red. Ask about me and your ears will ring with curses."

He laughed and finished his wine.

"My God," cried Gloster, "it makes me drunk when I think how the people curse me! Let men hate you if you want your heart to be warm."

They advanced into the garden, with Gloster striding unevenly in front, and Cailland said to von Emsdorf, "I'm not sure that I recognize him as Raskoi. Do you think he is real?"

"I can't tell," said von Emsdorf. "If he is a liar, and a spy, God help him, for I shall surely find out. How was his Russian accent?"

"Perfect, it seemed to me."

"I would have faith in him except that Louvain doesn't seem to recognize his face, and Louvain saw Raskoi in Russia. He's not sure, however, of the difference. . . . But I saw the beast handle my dog, today, the way a woman handles her favorite cat. When he was not thinking, with hands like the hands of a sculptor he touched the dog and the dog loved him. Now, Cailland, you are lending me the girl, are you not?"

"The girl?" echoed Cailland, alarmed.

"For a moment, only. She will not be broken to bits. We shall all be near," suggested von Emsdorf. "I know one thing, at least, and, by reputation, Raskoi with women is like a stallion among mares, or worse. If he is left with the girl and treats her as he treated the dog, with courtesy and tenderness, then I know that he is a pretender."

"We shall see," said Cailland, and he looked at the back of Gloster with narrowed eyes.

"Gleich, and you, di Parva, and Louvain—will you come with me?" said von Emsdorf. "Come with me and Cailland for a moment. I have something to show you in the rear garden."

They went straggling out as von Emsdorf said over his shoulder, "We return again in an instant, Gregor Raskoi!"

Lady Cecil was left behind.

"Ah hai!" said Gloster to the girl. "My father had a yearling filly that was as sleek as summer grass all year long. She never grew long hair and the winter cold made her tremble. But she was a lovely thing, like you. Like a fool, God let her die in her second winter and set us all cursing Him. But you are past your second winter. You have grown. Come and sit down beside me, my beautiful! There is a heel of Burgundy left in this bottle. Sit here!"

"I think . . ." said Lady Cecil, and made suddenly after the other men as Gloster sat down on a stone bench. He whirled in his place and caught her with a long arm.

"No, no, sweetheart!" shouted Gloster. "However fast you run, the rope can run faster! You are noosed! You are caught!" He caught her back onto the bench beside him.

"Willie, you're drunk and crazy!" gasped the girl.

"Fight, you fool!" said Gloster under his breath.

She raised her hand, thought twice, and struck him in the face.

"Ah, that's a good winter drink!" laughed Gloster. "Pepper in the beer! But I can drink it and never blink! You don't see tears in my eyes, my darling. . . . Again! Again! . . . Sweet hands! They fall on my face like flakes of snow; you are as cool as heaven on a summer's day; you are like the ice in the clouds, and I am hot with the dust of the damned journey. Come to my arms, my dear!"

He caught her into his lap.

"Are you crazy?" he whispered. "Fight! Fight! . . . Oh ho, my fine filly! How the oats have sleeked your flanks and put fire in your eyes and whitened your teeth; and how the good hay has sweetened your breath! Ah hai! There is no force in your hands! . . . Now I understand you. A woman in love is a fool and a slug in the grass; but a woman in hate can be felt. Hate me while I love you! Show your teeth while I kiss you. By God, I could keep you two years without growing tired. And I shall keep you. Oh ho, she kicks?

That is soon stopped, pretty legs. Do you think you make me angry? I am not one of the little Western people. I have spread my elbows from the Urals to the Baltic and still I could not stretch out my arms . . . but they are long enough to hold you. . . . Scream, Cecil, damn you!"

Jules Cailland and von Emsdorf had paused under the arches that led from the court garden to the open garden in the rear of the old building.

"Ah, there it is!" said von Emsdorf. "Now if an angel came down out of heaven and denied it, I would know that that is Raskoi. I have heard how he stables himself in Moscow and Leningrad. See the beast, Cailland . . . and do as you please to stop him."

Cailland was running toward the girl. He caught Gloster's shoulder and tried to draw the girl away in the middle of her scream.

"Hit me, jackass!" said Gloster.

Cailland groaned, stepped back, and struck Gloster heavily on the side of the head. The American let his arms fall away from the girl. He spilled back and lay on his back with his legs sticking into the air, held up by the stone bench.

Without making an effort to rise, all at once he began to laugh, heartily. Von Emsdorf and the others were running back toward him.

"Welcome, Mother Earth!" cried Gloster. "Dirty German feet have soiled you, but now the heart of a Russian lies on your breast. Do you receive me? Do you recognize your child? Does the mother womb remember me? Hail, mother! Hail!"

Von Emsdorf and Gleich took him by the arms and lifted him to his feet. A lump was growing at the edge of his hair near his left ear. He lifted the bottle and waved it.

"To our mother!" he yelled. He poured the rest of the

Burgundy down his throat.

"Gregor Raskoi," said von Emsdorf, smiling with a singular appreciation of this outbreak. "Raskoi, do you hear me?"

"Shout louder! Stand on your toes!" said Gloster. "My head is above the clouds. Fly up, up to me! Burst your lungs shouting."

"Raskoi," said von Emsdorf, "you are drunk. It is a pity, but you are drunk."

"Why do you pity me?" asked Gloster. "If I am drunk, God envies me. And you, little, whining animal, pretend to pity me?"

"You must go home, Raskoi," said von Emsdorf, sobering a little.

"I shall not go," said Gloster. "Now that I remember it, there is a pain on the side of my head. I have been hit by some fool who doesn't know that I shall murder him. Where is he? Oh God, what an itching there is in my hands for his throat!"

"He has run away," said von Emsdorf. "Now, you go home and find some more of that good red wine, and don't forget that we want you here at eight o'clock. But sleep some, Raskoi. Have a little sleep. Lie down and you will be asleep at the third breath."

"Although you are a German," said Raskoi, "there is a little sense in your brain. I shall go. Tonight I shall have him in my hands, shall I not?"

"Perhaps. Farewell, my friend," said von Emsdorf.

He looked after Gloster as the latter left the court and was met at the door by two servants who escorted him.

"Crazy, crazy!" said von Emsdorf. "But something magnificent about him, eh? Mademoiselle, do you forgive me? You have been mishandled. Perhaps he should have been horsewhipped. He shall be whipped if it happens that he gets out of hand again. . . . And yet something magnificent—out of the soil—ah, if German brains could direct those hands, a hundred and eighty million of them, we would rip the world apart and then remake it, piece by piece, after a new pattern!"

Chapter Twelve

But gloster went back to his hotel with the world spinning before his eyes, and that world was composed not of the faces of von Emsdorf and the others of his group, but of Cailland's half sneering, half suspicious look, and the wild bewilderment of Lady Cecil.

So, as he strode down the hall to his room, he was already grinding his teeth. He unlocked and closed the door behind him. He wanted to get the dirt of alcohol out of his brain, so went straight for the bathroom to douse his head in cold water. But when he entered the room he saw Elise sitting by the window smoking a cigarette. She was wearing an afternoon gown and the cloak which went with it lay over the arm of her chair. As she looked at him the black of her eyelashes joined the dark of her eyes and made them seem enormous.

"Ah," said Gloster. "Still here? Still tied to this?" He pointed to the closed door of the closet. The girl watched him without giving an answer.

He went into the bathroom and put his head under the cold tap of the washbowl. The water presently ran cold over the nape of his neck. It washed a stain out of his brain, soot

112

out of his eyes. It came rushing down across his eyes and nose and mouth, cutting off his breath. He sputtered. He drank of it.

When he turned off the tap and lifted his head a bath towel was passed over his shoulders. He kept his dripping head bowed. She gave his hair a rub with the ends of the towel and then twisted a hand towel around his head.

"You can lie down without ruining the pillow now," she told him. "Will you catch cold?"

"No, I won't catch cold," said Gloster.

"Lie down," said the girl. "I'll open a bed."

He went to the chair and fell back in it, closing his eyes. He could feel her coming near.

"Why don't you wear a decent perfume?" asked Gloster. "That thick, sweet stuff chokes me."

"It's in my handkerchief," she said. "I'm throwing it away. You can't smell it now."

"Take it out doors and take yourself with it," said Gloster. "Will you do that for me?" She sat down on the arm of his chair. "Will you go?" said Gloster. "And take a message for me to Winton Holling Jones."

"Yes," said the girl.

"Tell him that he can be damned, and his work can be damned, and all England can be damned along with him. Tell him that and give him my special regards. My special personal regards for a quick trip to hell and a hot spot in it. Will you tell him that?"

"Yes," said Elise.

"Start now, please," said Gloster.

She put her arm carefully around the towel which bandaged his head.

"Has it been pretty bad?" she asked.

"I don't want you or the talk or the touch of you," said Gloster. "Get out!"

113

She pulled his head gradually over on her shoulder, turning to him and cherishing his face, silently.

"Damnation!" sighed Gloster.

"It was a fist that put that lump on your head?" she asked.

"A rat of a lying, sneaking French cat," said Gloster. "He thumped me. I had to ask him to pop me. And then Gregor Raskoi—may he rot in hell—fell down on his back and laughed like a drunken fool, and raved about the Mother Earth, and had to be drawn up to his feet, and steadied like a beast."

"I know," said the girl, and he felt the strong shudder that went through her body. "Tell me more about it. Nothing will do you any good except talking."

"No. I'm going to sleep," said Gloster. "Don't move. I'm going to sleep. Can you sing?"

"Sotto voce, yes."

"Sotto voce, then."

She sang the little old German nursery song which runs like this:

> All the yellow sun
> All the blue sky
> The sweet May wind
> The red rose petals
> The soft white clouds
> Rolled up in one body
> And placed in my arms
> To hear my heart beat

"Don't be a fool," said Gloster. "Why are you sniveling?"

"I had one, once," she said.

"A baby?"

"Yes."

114

"Did you leave that in Russia, too?"

"Yes."

"Dead?"

"Yes."

He put his arm around her.

"Will you stop crying?" asked Gloster.

"Yes."

"Sing another song."

Her voice trembled, paused, and began softly and smoothly once more the weird old chant of the snake-charmers in Egypt, a strange sing-song as monotonous as the pulses of sleep itself.

All ye who crawl on your bellies:
All ye of the sixty-three kinds,
Listen to the voice of a friend.
Let there be peace between us.
Peace to you and to yours I swear;
Swear peace to me and to mine.
Out of your holes come forth,
Come forth all ye out of the grass
To look in my face and to swear.
I shall not harm you or yours;
You shall not harm me or mine
In the name of God, in the name of His prophet.

Gloster slept. After a time he began to groan in his sleep with every outgoing breath. The girl pushed his head back. She loosened his necktie, using her hands firmly and strongly and slowly, like one who knew all about sleepers. The groaning then stopped.

She remained perfectly still. The sun crawled across the chair in which they sat and a cool shadow took its place. She was cold, but she did not move. Once tears poured

115

into her eyes but she fought them back as though an eye were watching her.

Then someone tapped on the door of the living room.

She bit her lip, looking anxiously down at the face of the sleeper. The tap came again.

"Wake up!" said Elise. "Hush! There is someone at the door."

He pushed her away with both hands, looked at her a moment, and then stood up. "Go answer the door," said Gloster. "Give me thirty seconds."

He entered the living room before her, picked up a bottle of the Burgundy, knocked the head off the bottle, and went to the window, singing an old Tartar drinking song.

He let his voice swell a little at this moment, hearing the click of the opening door; but as he ran on with his song, his voice still swelling bigger, he felt the weight of the silence behind him, and the pressure of eyes.

He turned, waving the broken bottle of wine, and saw Lady Cecil standing in front of the door with her hand still holding the knob of it. He stared at her and then took a good swallow of the wine.

"Well?" he said. She watched him. He saw her swallowing, with a hard effort. "Sit down," said Gloster.

She walked over to a chair and stood beside it, still drinking him in. "I had to see you," she said.

"It's all right," said Gloster. "Don't be so damned stagy. She's in the know."

"I had to see you, Willie," she repeated.

"You had to take the chance of coming here? What if they followed you?"

"I knew it was a chance," she said.

"And you had to take it?"

"I had to see you," she said.

"You're not on a stage, darling," said Gloster. "Nobody's

116

going to encore any of these speeches."

Elise went into the bedroom.

"Come back," said Gloster. "I don't want you to go away."

She did not appear again.

"Are you going to be horrid?" asked Lady Cecil.

"I'm not horrid, De Waters," he said. "And as long as you have a good Norman name like that, why do you use such silly, girlish language? Why don't you talk out like a stout-hearted fellow, De Waters?"

"I'm going to talk out," said Lady Cecil.

He nodded. "I hope you will," he said. "You've come to say goodbye, haven't you?"

"Willie!"

"Well, what is it?"

"I don't mean to hurt you like this."

"Whom are you hurting? Don't talk nonsense."

"You can't deceive me, Willie. You look sick. Willie, forgive me!" She came to him with her hands out. He took both her wrists in one of his hands.

"Don't try to make an ass of me," he said. "Do I look pale to you? It's because I have a touch of damned indigestion. It takes me that way now and then. Too much Burgundy. Anybody will tell you that Burgundy is hell on the stomach. I mean, you can't swim in it, the way I've been doing."

"Willie, I do love you," said the girl.

"That's sweet of you," said Gloster. "But compared with Cailland. . . ."

"I have to tell you about him."

"Is he wonderful?"

She drew closer.

"Willie. I can dare to tell you. . . . You're the only single person that I dare to tell. He's Monsieur Jacquelin!"

"Is he?" said Gloster.

"Yes," she breathed.

"The poor devil!" said Gloster. "He's known you nearly a day and a half and you're already chattering his name all over the face of the world."

"Only to you, Willie."

"When did you find out that you loved him?" asked Gloster.

"You'll hate me when I say . . . It was when he rushed in and—separated us, today, Willie. Do you forgive me for saying that?"

"No. I love the truth. Did you hear what I said to him before he smacked me?"

"No. What did you say?"

"I've forgotten," said Gloster. "But Cailland has nerve. I beg your pardon. Monsieur Jacquelin has nerve."

"Do you know something, Willie? I think he really cares for me!"

"I'll bet your boots that he does."

"But really, Willie. For me! Isn't that miraculous?"

"When will you marry him?"

"As soon as I can love him, as he deserves to be loved."

"You're not temporizing, are you?"

"No. It's only—because I haven't known him long—and something comes up in me at the last moment and prevents me."

"He hasn't held you close enough; he hasn't said the right things," suggested Gloster.

"Willie, don't be sickening. Are you going to make me sorry that I've come? Will you be nice? Will you kiss me goodbye?"

"No," said Gloster.

"After all," she said, "you seem able to find comfort for yourself—of a certain sort."

118

"Of a certain sort?" said Gloster.

"Yes," she answered, lifting her head.

"Elise," he said.

The girl appeared at the door.

"Come here," said Gloster. "Her name is Elise. . . . Elise, this is Cecil. Funny name for a girl, isn't it? That's why she cut her hair so short. Elise, what do you think of her?"

Elise said nothing.

"She has ideas about you," said Gloster. "Maybe you have ideas about her. I'd like to have her hear them."

Elise said: "Will you come into the next room with me for a moment?"

"Yes. Of course," answered Lady Cecil.

They went into the bedroom.

"It isn't exactly the way you think," said Elise, very gently. "Not quite exactly. I could love Gloster if he wanted me to. But we have something else to think about. You see?"

She unlocked the door of the coat closet and pulled it open, slowly. Afterward she shut it and locked it once more. Lady Cecil, with a sick face, stood back by the first bed, resting her hand on the foot of it.

"I understand," she managed to say, and went back into the living room to Gloster.

She whispered to him. "Willie, you can't stay on here. They'll find it in a few hours. And then they'll catch you. Besides, von Emsdorf is still suspicious in spite of the crazy performance you made with me this afternoon. He's determined to watch you carefully. Willie, tell me that you'll go away!"

"Don't bother me," said Gloster. "Go back to your Frenchman."

"I have to go back to him," said the girl. "But don't you see, Willie, that there is no need for you, there is nothing that you can do? Do you think that he needs help?"

"No, I suppose he's invincible if he's Jacquelin," said Gloster.

"If only you could take off our minds the worry about you. That would be the greatest thing in which you could help," she told him.

"You begin to be a bore," said Gloster. "Run along, my dear, will you?"

"I won't go!" cried Lady Cecil. "Not till you've promised to leave Berlin at once. Willie, Willie, don't you see what you've done? There's the guilt of a murder hanging over your heads—you and Elise. Willie, will you please come to your senses and travel as far and as fast as airplanes will carry you?"

He took her inside his arm, opened the door of the room, and pushed her into the hall. "The elevators are yonder," said Gloster, and closed the door.

"What were we talking about?" Gloster asked Elise.

"Nothing that I can remember," she answered.

"Why did you come here?" he asked.

"Vaguely to try to be of some help. Particularly to try to keep maids and things away from the closet," said Elise.

"You're one of the good ones," said Gloster, sitting down again. "I'm as fresh as though I'd had a good night."

"What do we do next?" asked the girl.

"I go back to dinner at the von Emsdorf house, and then I look around and see what can be done. One of the great questions is: Has he photostated the plans and distributed them among his allies? What you do, I don't know. Will you stay here?"

"Probably."

"Elise, what did you think of my lady?"

"Is she going to break your heart?" asked Elise.

"I'm asking that of you."

"She's lovely," said the girl.

"That's no answer," said Gloster.

"She'll break your heart, I suppose," said Elise.

"Why will she? I'm a free white American, of age. I refuse to break my heart about her."

"You can't help it," said Elise. "She's got a touch of boy in her. Just a dash of independence and spirit; and men can't stand that. It knocks them over. It knocks them dizzy. She tries to treat you like a brother even when you're making love to her, doesn't she?"

"Is she a type?" asked Gloster.

"No, thank God," said Elise. "If there were ten more like her, men would never look at creatures like me."

The door opened behind them. Winton Jones came in, taking off his hat and closing the door gently behind him.

Chapter Thirteen

THE LITTLE man wore gray flannels and a shirt of thinnest gray wool with a fine blue stripe in it, and gray suede shoes, and yellow chamois gloves, so often washed that they were almost white. In his left hand he carried his straw hat and a stick of burnished malacca, the dark sort which has been smoked in the curing and is a deeper shade than mahogany. His body was extremely dapper and young. It was like the body of a fourteen- or fifteen-year-old boy, quick and supple, but on top of it was set the philosopher's great dome of a head, with the face peering out inhumanly through the big, darkened lenses of the glasses like a ship's brain through two ports.

"Ah, Elise," he said. "And my dear Mr. Gloster! But wait a moment. Raskoi, should I call you?" He looked at the clothes of Gloster. "I beg your pardon, Gregor Raskoi!"

"I thought you stayed at home?" said Elise, amazed. "I never knew that you went so far afield, Mr. Jones!"

"Oh, I have a dash here and there for the fun of it," answered Winton Holling Jones. "What are you doing with that broken bottle of wine, if you please?"

"That's the way the Russian animal is apt to take his

122

Burgundy," said Gloster.

"You put him out of the way, I suppose?" said Jones. "What on earth did you amateurs do? Drug him and leave him tied hand and foot in the bathroom?"

"Show him, Elise," said Gloster.

But Jones broke out, "No, you didn't do that! You were even greater fools! You killed him, Gloster?"

"No, I did," said the girl.

Winton Jones threw out a hand as though to protest. Then he allowed the arm to fall limply back against his side. "What happened?" he asked.

"I made acquaintance with Raskoi at the Landsberg Station," said Gloster. "He invited me to get drunk with him at this hotel. The other things followed on. He was bashed over the head with a bottle. I thought I had taken Elise completely out of it, but I was wrong. She came back like a duck to a decoy. That's about all, except that I'm being Raskoi for the sake of von Emsdorf and his partners."

"You, Elise?" asked Winton Jones.

"Raskoi managed to pick me up on the train," she said. "I came here and then a lot of things were about to happen to me when Mr. Gloster appeared."

"You've smashed my work to bits," said Winton Jones without the least violence. "You've given us a definite time limit. I think we may have had a ghost of a chance, up to this point, but now we lose all chances whatever. Before morning, the body will be found. Where is it? In a closet?"

"Yes," said Gloster.

"A pair of children!" murmured Winton Jones, closing his eyes. "Children! Perfect and absolute children! God forgive me for sending a baby like you into such work as this, Elise, but I thought that there was enough Russian hate in you to sharpen your brains. What happened? Did you lose your head about Gloster?"

"Not then," said Elise.

"Afterward?" asked Jones.

She looked at Gloster and said nothing.

"Do you know," said the gentle, thoughtful voice of Jones, "that this may set back the progress of the world a hundred years? Interesting, when you think about it that way. Charlotte Corday did very well with her knife; but it was nothing compared with what my dear Elise did with her bottle. The sling of David was utterly ineffective compared with the bottle of Elise. Dear Elise, you will be immortal, of course. And the Germans soon will send you to the heaven you deserve."

"Talk to me," said Gloster. "Don't concentrate on her."

"My dear Gloster, you are an American," said Winton Jones, "and I'm afraid that I lack your dialect—lingo, do you say?—for expressing myself."

"Go on," said Gloster. "Go ahead. Be English. Show us why the whole world loves an Englishman. What the devil were we to do?"

Winton Jones sprang to his feet. He kept his voice low, but the effect was as though he had blown a trumpet.

"You were to obey orders!" he exclaimed. "You were sent out with perfectly precise instructions. Both of you were ordered to trail him, not to murder him. You were to let him lead you to the place where he was to meet the others. Now the chance is lost. We'll have no guide. We're lost in the dark, fumbling toward von Emsdorf."

"I'm dining with von Emsdorf this evening," said Gloster, "and the other three will be there."

"Dining? Von Emsdorf? And the rest? Do you mean that you've passed yourself off as Raskoi even with von Emsdorf?" cried Winton Jones.

"There's plenty of animal in me, Jones," said Gloster. "I merely have to pour it out, and sing a Russian song or two.

It's true that he's suspicious. Suspicious as the very devil. Louvain, the Belgian, has been in Russia and did not recognize my face. However, I gave them a little show with a good deal of local color today, and now they feel surer of me, though at any moment the ice may break under my feet."

Jones was on his small feet, walking rapidly up and down.

"Von Emsdorf. All of them. In the same house with them. This is glorious luck, Gloster!" he said.

"Luck?" said Elise.

"Cleverness, cleverness, cleverness, if you will," said Jones. "And for a novice, I can't see how you managed to do it. I really can't! The extraordinary courage of a beginner . . . We'll work out a plan of action."

"Cailland. Have you seen Cailland in Berlin?" asked Gloster.

"The Frenchman? Is he here?"

"He is. It appears that he admits he is Monsieur Jacquelin," said Gloster.

"Admits it? The man wouldn't be fool enough to do that," declared Winton Jones.

"It's an impressive role to play in front of a woman," said Gloster.

"What woman?" asked Jones.

"Lady Cecil," said Gloster.

"She here also?" asked Jones.

"She is. In the same hotel with Cailland."

The names came slowly off Jones' tongue: "Cailland—Cecil—Elise—Gloster . . . How in the name of God can we work all those elements together and make one strength for our work?"

The telephone rang. Gloster answered it.

"Gloster?" called a familiar voice.

"Is it you, Cailland?"

"Yes," said the Frenchman. "The devil is to pay. Von Emsdorf knows that Cecil went to see you at the hotel. Watch yourself, Gloster. Watch yourself! Von Emsdorf is suspicious all over again. He can't imagine any reason why the girl should come to see you. You'd better be equipped with reasons before you appear at the house this evening. Is that clear? Goodbye."

Gloster hung up the telephone.

"Cailland is playing on our side of the fence, at least," he said. "He warns us that von Emsdorf knows that Cecil has visited me here today."

"You should not have come," said Jones.

"That's behind us and done," remarked Gloster. "What's the next step to go? Have you got it in your head, Jones?"

"Von Emsdorf is the target," said Jones. "We have to decide now what sort of a bullet is most likely to hit him."

CHAPTER FOURTEEN

JULES CAILLAND, as the day ended, sat in front of the mirror in his room alone with his thoughts. Yet he never found himself really alone when he had his own image for company, and in the triple mirror of the dressing table he found his face revealed twice in profile and once in full face. His physiognomy remained to Cailland a perpetual interest. The roughness with which the features were hewn gave them all the more distinction at a little distance. A finer polish would, of course, be preferable for close social contacts, but whenever Cailland thought of himself it was at a distance from the ordinary man, elevated as upon a pedestal, removed from the most dusty concerns of common man.

When Cailland found himself in difficulties, it was his habit to retire to a room and look upon his own face because he had such a gift of inner perception that he could see in it, always, only that which was best. He perceived God's intention rather than the mundane fact.

Now he roughed up his hair, suddenly, and gave himself the effect of one who was running against a high wind. He waited for his mind to speed up in an equal degree, and

127

when this did not happen, he leaned back in his chair and sighed with a mild unhappiness.

He could not really be discontented when he had his image for company and if he had had at that moment a glass of good wine he would have felt that the world was going on at an excellent pace indeed. It was his rule, in these times of great decisions, to look at himself first and to find his ideas by the inspiration of his own face. Since the ideas were slow in coming, he altered his expression at once.

It was a time of the highest danger, therefore he thrust out his chin with resolution. When he observed himself in three-quarter view, lifting his chin a little, half closing his eyes, he was like some early god, some Prometheus who had brought the fire to man and now endured the divine torment for his greatness of heart.

If he bowed his head, the philosopher appeared in that weighty brow. If he frowned, fear almost started into his own heart. In short, he could study himself endlessly, and always with good results.

Now, sitting at this telephone, he got the room he was calling, at last, and the voice of Lady Cecil came sweetly to him.

"Ah, Cecil," he said, "how your voice fills up the whole, great hollow world! The lonely world, Cecil. How alone I have been! How empty and alone . . . alone!"

"Are you to be a poet also, Jules?"

"It's when the day ends," said Cailland "that I feel it. I can get through the day with this or with that, but when the day ends, between daylight and darkness there is a deep horizon through which I want to escape into a new life, a true life, a real life, Cecil."

He roughed up his hair, as he said this, and admired in the front glass and the side glass the windy effect of emo-

128

tion which this produced in his aspect.

"We mustn't talk of such things," said the girl. "If you speak of loneliness, Jules, do you think I'm very happy, with the day dying in my room? I want to tell you an interesting bit that I heard today."

"What is it?"

"The real Monsieur Jacquelin—"

"Ha?" cried Cailland, starting violently.

"Wait!" she urged. "The real Monsieur Jacquelin is called Djecklen, and he's a Czech. Silly, isn't it?"

Cailland laughed, freely and heartily. "You are going to von Emsdorf's place tonight?" she asked.

"Yes."

"Will you be careful of yourself?" begged Lady Cecil. "Will you try to be very careful?"

"Why do you say it, Cecil?" asked Cailland. "When a man puts his head into the lion's mouth, beg the lion to be careful, but not the man!"

"Ah, Jules. I know!" said the girl. "When this business is ended, will you give it up forever?"

Cailland stared at himself in the glass, and sighed. "Don't you see, Cecil," he explained, "that if life is a flower, adventure is the fragrance of it? Subtract danger from existence, and what is left? A stale, dead, unprofitable thing. I'd as soon sit down and read about events as not to be a part of them!" He said this with appropriately large gestures.

"There's nothing I can say. I know," said the girl.

"There's nothing you can say that is not music to me," he answered. "Tell me, Cecil, why you went to see Gloster today?"

"I wanted to tell him that he was overdoing his part," she answered. "And I wanted to say goodbye to him, Jules."

129

"Ah?" said Cailland. Joy closed his eyes and interrupted his voice.

"I had to say goodbye to him," said the girl.

"Cecil, you have loved him?" he asked.

"I still love him, I'll always love him," said Lady Cecil.

"But—" he suggested.

"Ah, it isn't an unqualified love, now," she answered. "So I had to tell him, and say goodbye to him. He's so simple . . . and so wild and so brave, Jules. And there's something good and full-hearted about him, don't you think so?"

"I think you're adorable," said Jules Cailland. "Will you come down here?"

"No, Jules."

"I have something to tell you."

"I mustn't come to your room."

"I want to tell you the story you were asking about," said Cailland.

"You mean," she said, "about Alexander's marriage?"

"Yes."

"I'm hungry to hear it!"

"Then come to me, Cecil."

"Jules, I simply mustn't."

"If you cared for me, Cecil. . . ."

"I do care for you, Jules."

"Ah, but not much."

"That's not true."

"And still you won't come?"

"I mustn't. But oh, how I want to hear about the king's marriage! Goodbye, Jules."

The receiver clicked at the other end of the line, and Cailland, smiling and frowning at the same time, slowly put up the instrument. He observed his windy hair in the glass and found there, to his surprise, not only the two large images of himself but also a third face that drifted slowly towards the glass from the distant direction of the door. It was a dim light that lived in the room, by this time, and the features of the face that moved toward him were obscured as though by a mist. Even through that dimness Cailland guessed enough to make him leap to his feet and gasp out: "Jacquelin!"

"Sit down," said Monsieur Jacquelin.

Cailland collapsed into his chair, with his back to his visitor. He sat there with his fists pressed against his face and his head thrown back, whispering: "Jacquelin, why have you come? Why have you come? Are you angry, Jacquelin?"

Jacquelin moved on until he was immediately behind Cailland. In this position, the Frenchman was unable to see the reflection of the other higher than the shoulders; so he was left without that intimate guide, the study of the face which speaks.

"Have you sold yourself to von Emsdorf?" asked Jacquelin.

"He gave me only what he owed me for the stealing of the plans."

"How much did he pay you?"

"A few thousands."

"You sit taller in your chair and you stand bigger in your world," said Jacquelin. "How many thousands did he pay you?"

"Jacquelin . . ."

"Tell me!"

"Seventy thousand dollars."

"That is enough to buy your soul," said Jacquelin.

"No, no!" cried Cailland. "He bought nothing. I have not broken my promises. Just now I have been sending a warning—as you know. . . ."

"If von Emdorf's plans succeed, you would have the world before you, Cailland."

"Jacquelin . . ."

"Well?"

"I think it may be true. He may bring the world to his feet. Suppose that we work together? You and I together, as it was in the old days? Jacquelin, time has passed over me. When you left me, all the glow went out of the world. I found myself dropped down among little men again. There was nothing of importance. When I began to write the articles for *La Liberté* it wasn't really with the purpose of injuring you, but it was because I was vain. I was a fool. I wanted to show the world that I once had been attached to great things, even to Jacquelin himself. Do you understand that? But give me a chance to work with you, Jacquelin, and you'll find that you can trust me now!"

"I think I can, in part," said Jacquelin. "I intend to—in part."

"Will you . . ." cried Cailland, starting to rise from his chair.

"Sit still," said Jacquelin.

Cailland sank back into his place, straining his eyes upward as if by chance he could have a glimpse of the face of Jacquelin in the mirror.

"Go back to your hopes in von Emsdorf," said Jacquelin. "The push can go through. Von Emsdorf can have the world at his feet unless he is checked now. And you can be a great man. But if you continue to wear my name, before very long he is sure to find out that you are not what you pretend. What would he do then?"

"He would . . . I don't know."

"There's no mercy in him," said Jacquelin. "If he discovered that you had made a fool of him, ask yourself what he would do?"

132

"Stamp on me!" said Cailland.

"Certainly," said Jacquelin.

"But if you and I worked together with him and for him . . . Jacquelin, you and I could both be like kings!"

"I stand on the other side."

"Immovable?" groaned Cailland.

"Their first intention is the ruin of France. She is your country, Jules."

"She is worn out," answered Cailland. "France is dying. We only forestall the future, Jacquelin."

"Cailland!" said Jacquelin. Cailland buried his face in his hands again. "It would be the death of democracy," said Jacquelin. "It would be the undoing of a thousand years of history." Cailland was silent. "But von Emsdorf and the others can be stopped now," said Jacquelin, "if we can steal back the Maginot plans. Tonight."

"Suppose that we locate the hiding place of the plans—suppose that we actually are able to leave the house with them, what do we accomplish? We run for our lives. Von Emsdorf reaches out after us. We reach England, say. And what then? A pat on the back from Holling Jones. The plans are filed in a safe place. And we—we are forgotten! Jacquelin, I know that you care nothing about money and you will do without newspaper fame; but there are weaker and warmer bits of humanity in me! I can't rival you. I can't imitate you! You ask me to take a risk of a single chance in a hundred, and in the end to gain nothing whatever!"

"Cailland, you must make up your mind," said Jacquelin. "You are the trusted man in von Emsdorf's house. Without you, we can do nothing. You are our point of contact. Do you hear me?"

Cailland heard, and groaned again.

"There is a reward for you," said Jacquelin, at last. He

sighed and went on: "There is the girl, Cailland."

"She will never have me," said Cailland, shaking his head. "It's the name of Jacquelin that she had fallen in love with. I am nothing to her. She comes to me with her eyes shining, but when she is near me, the moment I stop talking about the past, she turns cold again."

"If she sees you being the lion in this work," said Jacquelin, "won't she give up the last scruple?"

"Do you mean," asked Cailland, throwing up his head suddenly, "that you would support me all the way through and then make it appear that the credit was mine? Would you make that stand in her eyes?"

"I mean exactly that," said Jacquelin.

"You would let her come to me?" repeated Cailland, amazed.

"I would give up my father and mother and my brothers," said Jacquelin, "to stop the work of von Emsdorf."

"Will you give me your hand?"

"It is here for you," said Jacquelin, and held it out to the Frenchman.

Chapter Fifteen

Von emsdorf said, "Truth, Cailland, is what we are trying to demonstrate to an unprepared world at the present moment—the inevitable truth that the *Deutsche Kultur* is the mind and soul of the future. Truth cuts with a sharp steel edge. Is the world able to endure this operation? We cannot tell. At least it is going to receive the shock and without a previous anaesthetic.'

Cailland said, merely, "I believe you, von Emsdorf."

The sharp eyes of the Prussian searched him through and through. "You seem a little nervous."

"Herr von Emsdorf, I am always nervous," said Cailland.

"Always?"

"How can one focus all of one's faculties on a bright point," asked Cailland, "without a touch of nerves? It is impossible."

Von Emsdorf studied this for a moment. "In Russia men are different. . . . But I mustn't keep you too long from Raskoi. I'm pleased that the two of you happened to come before the rest of the guests, and I've drawn you away from him for this moment to tell you what is in my mind. Or can you guess?"

"You were suspicious of Raskoi this afternoon. You're still suspicious," suggested Cailland. "You want me to draw him out this evening, because you think that the Russian may have something concealed in his mind."

Von Emsdorf tapped his fingers rapidly against the edge of the table behind which he sat as behind a desk. "You guess almost too well, Cailland," he said.

Cailland shrugged. "You know, Herr von Emsdorf, that I will not be talked to like a little boy."

"Naturally not," agreed von Emsdorf. "But you are right. I want you to watch Raskoi."

"What is in your mind about him?"

"A small thing. And yet not so small, either. That dog—that Friedrich der Grosse—is a peculiar beast. It has no love for anything in the world. It obeys me only because I taught it with a whip. And yet I saw it come to the hand of a drunken beast of a Russian! Odd, Cailland—terribly odd!"

"Afterward," said Cailland, "I saw the Russian treat a woman as only a Raskoi would attempt to do it. A beast pure and simple."

"It sticks in my mind," said von Emsdorf, "that all the rest may be beautiful acting. Such acting as only you, Cailland, might be considered capable of. Because when Raskoi extended his hand to that dog, Cailland, it was the instinctive and casual gesture of a man who did not know, really, what he was doing. Only the subconscious was speaking through that gesture, and the dog responded to it."

Cailland nodded.

"The subconscious is the real man," said von Emsdorf, thinking his way through his words. "And when I saw that slight act between the dog and the man, I knew that I was seeing the man's real soul. But how can that be the real soul of Raskoi, who flogged the horse to death which he was riding in Siberia, and flung a dog from a tenth story

136

window in Moscow?"

"True," nodded Cailland.

"Watch him," said von Emsdorf. "I have talked on the telephone with Stalin in Moscow and have his description of Raskoi in detail. But the description seems to fit in very well with the man who is here in Berlin. I've made one other step. I've ventured to have a real Russian brought into the house this evening as one of the servants. You'll notice him. Short, stocky, with a dark face. He will talk with Raskoi in Russian. He will force Raskoi into the use of words that only a real Russian can pronounce perfectly. That will be my final test and when it is made, if Raskoi passes, then he is Raskoi!"

Von Emsdorf stood up.

"Go back to him, Cailland," he said. "And use your eyes, carefully. The servants are watching him now but when you rejoin him they will leave you alone. That may make him spread his elbows at the board. Do your best to bring him out."

Cailland returned to the library where he found Gloster walking up and down the room in his suit of soiled tweed, waving the bottle to punctuate an impromptu speech which he was making, as though in rehearsal for a polemic to be delivered in front of a crowd of Russian workers.

"And as for the capitalistic nations," Gloster was saying, "as for the swallowers up of opportunity, the engrossers of money, the devourers of chance, we will teach them that there is only one picture of the ideal citizen of the great world state and that is a man in overalls, a grease pot in one hand and a monkey wrench in the other. That is the sort of picture that God wants to see on this earth. . . ."

"Well?" said Cailland, as he entered the room.

A servant was working at the fireplace, arranging the logs. Another replaced books on the shelves. A third stood by the door in readiness for orders.

The brows and the intellectual alertness of the three faces were not suggestive of the servant caste.

"Well," said Cailland, "will they vote for a speech like that?"

Gloster laughed loudly.

"The fools will vote for just that sort of a speech," he said.

A fourth servant approached the one at the door. A signal passed. The man at the fire and the one at the books began to withdraw, quietly.

"Will the workers like that speech?" repeated Cailland.

"I think," said Gloster, "that vodka is good but it burns the tongue and the belly. And Burgundy is better."

"Is that what you think about political systems?" asked Cailland, laughing.

"What else is there to think?" asked Gloster. "We build the high temple of thought today and tomorrow kicks it down into the dust, and the next day uses the building stones to pave the road. Wine, Cailland . . . wine is the only thinking, as a good Frenchman ought to know."

The servants had withdrawn now.

Cailland said, quietly, "I've been called to talk with von Emsdorf."

"Keep your voice up," said Gloster. "If you talk too softly, they'll notice the silence. Talk loudly, and they'll hear the noise without being able to make out the words."

"Von Emsdorf is devilishly suspicious."

"Why?" asked Gloster.

"The dog, there, lying under the desk in the corner. It seems that the beast was taught only to obey von Emsdorf and his whip; but it came to your hand at lunch and seemed to like your touch. That was out of character for a Raskoi. Von Emsdorf was amazed."

138

"Kindness always amazes a Junker," said Gloster. "It's a quality they leave in the region of the mind and never condescend to practice."

"He spoke about the subconscious," said Cailland.

"German again," said Gloster. "They have to make a mystery out of physical character, just as they have to reduce heaven to mathematics. They try to produce a common mean of thought and let nothing get above an average German approach. Your German," said Gloster expanding, "is an exploiter."

"Not so loud," cautioned Cailland.

"What difference does it make if they hear me? The more I disagree with their ideas the more crazy they will think I am, and all Russians are crazy to the Germans."

"Let's get back to the dog."

"The dog came to my hand, therefore at heart I am a gentle fellow; the dog recognized my gentleness; therefore I cannot be Raskoi."

"That's it."

"It's strange," said Gloster, "that he should be right."

"But are you really a gentle fellow?" asked Cailland, staring at him.

"I'm an American," said Gloster, "and all Americans are sentimental fools."

"From the European viewpoint?" suggested Cailland.

"Exactly."

"We're still five minutes ahead of the time when the other guests will arrive," said Cailland. "I've one other warning to give you. Von Emsdorf has employed for the evening a Russian who will appear as a servant. Short, stocky, dark. He'll talk Russian to you and see if your pronunciation is correct. Can you pass that test?"

"Nobody can who hasn't been born in Russia and lived there twenty years."

139

"Then go home now!" exclaimed Cailland.

"I'll go home when I have to."

"Gloster, you're more than half crazy."

"We're all crazy in spots," said Gloster. "This happens to be my spot. We've got five minutes left. Let's use it?"

"On what?" asked Cailland.

"On finding the Maginot plans."

Cailland laughed.

"Search the entire house of von Emsdorf?" he asked. "Search it in five minutes?"

"We'll never have another opportunity," said Gloster. "You're turned loose with me and the servants withdrawn so you can try me out at your own leisure. Five minutes— four minutes left. Where shall we search, Cailland?"

"God knows," said the Frenchman. "Where would you say?"

"Well, I'm subjected to temptation, under your eye," said Gloster. "Therefore I suppose the thing that might tempt me—if I'm a spy—must be fairly near."

"What do you mean?" asked Cailland.

"In this room," said Gloster.

"In this room? What?"

"The plans, I suppose," said Gloster, staring around him. "Three minutes and a half left. Find them for me, Cailland!"

"It's madness even to try. Even if the place were not plastered with servants. The plans might be lying back of any of those books in the shelves. We'd have to move every book to find out."

"Not as bad as that," said Gloster. "Not nearly as bad as that. Is there any pointer that indicates the right direction?"

"Not that I can see. The whole room is in perfect order," said Cailland.

"Nothing wrong?"

"No," said Cailland. "Not that I've noticed."

"There's the dog, though," said Gloster.

"The dog? What about Friedrich der Grosse?"

"Why should he be lying under the desk?"

"Because he likes the darkness of a corner."

"A dog ought to be with the man he's used to even if he doesn't love the man. But Friedrich der Grosse prefers to lie here in the library alone with two strangers. Remember that even the voice of a strange man is a torment to a dog's ears. But Friedrich der Grosse remains on his spot."

"I've given you the explanation," said Cailland.

"Ever hear of a dog staying on a spot even when he didn't want to?"

"Yes, if he's put on guard," answered Cailland.

"Cailland, walk to the desk and see what happens."

Cailland stared a few seconds at his companion, then rose and walked toward the desk.

Friedrich der Grosse watched him across the room with yellow-green eyes, then rose suddenly and snarled. The hair lifted along his back as he glared at Cailland.

The Frenchman halted.

"He's a devil!" said Cailland, going back a step.

"Not at all," said Gloster. "He's doing his duty. He'd snarl at anybody in the world, I suppose, except at his master. It's the desk he's guarding. Therefore the plans are in the desk."

"Nonsense!" said Cailland. "There must be a steel safe in this house and the plans will be in the safe."

"Not at all," said Gloster. "Von Emsdorf is not such a fool as to hide such a great thing in a place certain to be searched. He'll hide it more or less in the open, I'm sure. And the desk is fairly open. There aren't even any secret compartments in it, I'll lay my money."

141

"But what can we do?" asked Cailland, frowning. "My God, Gloster, I think you've hit on the thing. But how does that help us?"

"We still have two minutes."

"If we go near the desk, the dog growls. If the dog makes a noise, the servants will come."

"I'm going to use some of that good nature and kindness that von Emsdorf suspected in me," said Gloster. "Watch!"

He rose, singing, walked carelessly across the room, pulled a book off a shelf, and went with it toward the desk.

Friedrich der Grosse rose again to his feet, bristling. Gloster held out his hand and laid it on the head of the wolf-dog. Friedrich der Grosse whined and licked the hand.

"Dogs don't love von Emsdorf and his whip," said Gloster. "Friedrich der Grosse likes people who are not afraid of him."

He looked over the drawers of the desk without haste.

"Get away from it!" exclaimed Cailland, in an agony. "I've just heard somebody come from the street into the front hall."

"I've still a few seconds," said Gloster, and pulled open the largest drawer.

On top he saw a pile of neatly titled ledgers, such as a German housekeeper would use to store with accounts, patient generation after generation. He lifted the entire pile and from beneath drew out two thick envelopes large enough to take typewritten manuscripts. He opened and peered into one of these before he replaced the ledgers and closed the drawer.

"I have it," said Gloster, and crossed the room again to the shelves.

He put back the books he had taken down and behind the lowest and largest range of books he dropped the two envelopes, side by side.

142

"In the name of God," whispered Cailland, "have you really found it?"

"I have," said Gloster.

"But what good will it do to leave them there?" asked Cailland.

"I don't know," said Gloster. "It merely means that we know, for the moment, where the plans are. And von Emsdorf does not."

"But when he searches the library?"

"Will he? At once? Perhaps not," said Gloster. "He's more apt to search his guests if he misses the plans this evening."

Footsteps came through the next room. Gloster pulled another book from the shelves as young Gleich came into the room.

"Look, Austrian!" shouted Gloster. "Here is a book about Napoleon! I know it by his picture in the front. And here is a picture of Emperor Alexander the First. Is it a book about Austerlitz? Is it a book telling how the Frenchman thrashed you? By God, what a blessing for Europe Austria has been. The punching bag that's kept the real countries of the world in good condition!"

CHAPTER SIXTEEN

ELISE, WALKING up and down through the hotel living room of Gregor Raskoi, heard not a sound, but a fresher draft of wind blew suddenly through the window and when she turned in her walking she saw four men in police uniform entering the door.

The lieutenant at their head was a gray man with a head so closely clipped that the scalp shone pink through the bristles.

"Fräulein?" he said.

She stood still and watched the four. "Well?" she asked.

"We shall be engaged here for a short time," said the lieutenant. "Don't let us disturb you. Anton. Johann. Wilhelm. Take the other room first."

The three disappeared into the bedroom. The lieutenant sat down. "Be seated Fräulein," he said. "And have a cigarette with me. *Nein?*"

"Why not?" asked Elise, smiling on him.

"You know Herr Raskoi well?" asked the lieutenant.

"I know him for a day and a half," said Elise. "But quite well!"

"A good Russian?" asked the lieutenant.

144

"Did you ever know a good Russian?" she asked.

The lieutenant looked at her again. Then he laughed. From the other room came the noise of opening drawers, opening and closing doors.

"But still you know him?" asked the lieutenant.

"Not very well," she said. "It's my wish not to know men too well. . . . Why have you come here?" asked the girl.

"Do you care?" he responded.

"I? Not a bit!" she said.

"You don't care if Herr Raskoi falls into a little trouble?"

"I hope it's a trouble that makes the Russian in him sweat. . . . Oh, that would be nice to see!"

"Hmm!" murmured the lieutenant, smiling. "The world ripens a woman. Life in the world ripens her. It is like the summer sun for flowers, etc."

"Thank you, Herr Leutnant," said Elise, also smiling. There was a distinct crash inside as a door was pried open. "Are they going to break up the furniture?" asked the girl, reclining on the couch.

"Nothing we are not prepared to pay for," said the lieutenant.

One of the Schupos appeared in the bedroom doorway and saluted. "Ah?" said the lieutenant.

"Herr Leutnant," said the policeman.

The lieutenant rose, bowed to the girl, and saluted her. "Ten seconds—pardon me," he said, and marched into the bedroom. Elise cast one glance at the door, another toward the window. Then, gradually, she composed herself and leaned back on the couch again. She was smiling through a cloud of cigarette smoke when the lieutenant came back into the room with a slow step. He was rubbing his hands together as though he were washing them clean.

"This Raskoi, you have only been with him for a day and a half?" he asked.

"That's all. Though I might call it a year and a half," said Elise.

"A good, quiet man most of the time?"

"Perhaps, when he's not drunk, but he's always drunk," said Elise.

"Has he ever been violent with you?" asked the lieutenant.

She put her hand quickly to her side. "No," she said, after an instant. "No, not very."

"I see," said the lieutenant, gently. "Where is he now?"

"He'll be back in a moment," she said.

"Truly—in a moment?"

"Yes," said Elise.

"You don't know where he is?"

"Down in the bar, I suppose. I could find him."

"Ah, could you? If he's not in the bar would you know the next place to look?"

"Why, yes. I suppose so. I could almost trace him. By the smell!" She wrinkled her nose in disgust.

The lieutenant started and then smiled very broadly. "Suppose you go find him and bring him up here?" he said.

"Why not?" asked Elise.

She paused at the door.

"Just some old friends who have dropped in to see him?" she suggested.

"Ah, exactly," said the lieutenant. "Just some old friends who have come all the way from Moscow to see him! You'll remember? All the way from Moscow."

She drew in her breath through her teeth. "I hope you have to use a whip on him!" she said.

"But maybe we shall have to use our boots on him first," said the lieutenant. "Or gun butts? Would you care?"

"May I stay and watch?" she asked.

"Sweetheart!" said the lieutenant.

He was laughing as she went out into the hallway.

146

"Burgundy! Burgundy! Burgundy!" shouted Gloster. "No more of this filthy wash—this champagne—this white nothing with bubbles in it! I would not give it to a dog! I would not water sheep with it, not if I wanted to cut good wool from them later. Here, you, move your feet, wake up, use your hands, get me Burgundy!"

Behind Gloster's chair, at the dinner table, stood a man much shorter than the others who were serving the guests. He was stocky and dark, with a red color shining through his cheeks.

"I go at once, sir," he said, in Russian.

"Let me look at you," said Gloster in the same tongue. Then he broke into German to say, "Where did you find the color that was put in your cheeks? What did you pay for it?"

"God gave it to me, sir," said the servant.

"You lie," shouted Gloster. "You paid good money for it."

"Not I," insisted the servant.

"Do you hear?" roared Gloster, leaning back in his chair. "The filthy rascal admits everything. He admits that he has worked for a master with a good cellar of wine. He has not paid for his drinking. No, not he. But search his dirty pockets and you'll find that he has in them a good imitation of the wine cellar key. In the cold of the night he goes down into the cave. He looks around him at the stacks of bottles. Saliva runs hot into his mouth. He swallows and blesses himself. Where shall he begin? Oh, sun of France, oh blood red sun that cherishes the good grapes of Burgundy and makes them fat and sweet! Oh sun of France that ever your good wine should go to hearten such a thief as this one! Look at his face and see the lie written there! Wine, wine, wine! Only the juice of the grape could put such color in a human face."

147

He lifted his fist and turned in his chair. The servant stood still and smiled with stupid, steadfast eyes, waiting for the blow.

"No, Raskoi!" called von Emsdorf.

"Damn you and what you say," answered Gloster. "I am at your table, am I not? I am guest, am I not? And can I not beat one of your servants if I choose? Ah-ha, it is plain that there is no hospitality in this land! Fat, stupid, sweating Germany, there is no wit or brain in you! Ah, if you were in my Moscow house and wished to strike a servant, I would only stop you to put a whip in your hand. Would I not, you dog?"

"Yes, master," said the Russian.

"*He* knows me," said Gloster. "Here, fool. Give me your hand. Do you feel the strength in that hand? If you were mine, I would use that strength to take you by the hair of the head, for a wine thief. Tell me, you rascal, are you not a thief?"

"I am nothing in the world except what you say," said the servant, bowing over the great hand of Gloster.

"Well," said Gloster, "have you anything to say for yourself?"

"I have no words except what you give me, master," said the servant in Russian.

"Keep the words and use them to damn yourself in hell!" said Gloster. "Get out of my sight and never come back again unless you're carrying a bottle of good red Burgundy in each hand. Go, go before I throw something. Quickly, thief!"

"I should keep you to find out the thieves in my house," said von Emsdorf, smiling at Gloster.

"Thieves?" said Gloster. "We are all thieves. Mankind divides into two parts and portions. One is a great part. The other is a very, very, very small part. The great part of men are stupid thieves. The small, small, small part is composed of the clever thieves. I hope to God that everybody at this table is a clever thief, or else our business will go to hell. I am myself a very good thief. I smile in your face and kiss you while I pick your pocket. I kneel for the priest's blessing and come away with his golden cross, and curse him if it turns out to be nothing but silver gilt.

"When I think what a thief I am, I thank the God that made me. Ah-hai, Emsdorf, I am not very drunk. I am only happy when I think what a great thief God made when He made me. And I thank Him, and call Him brother."

Outside the dining room, Nicolai, the Russian, found himself alone in the hall that led to the pantry and ventured to open the hand into which that drunken guest had pressed a bit of paper.

"My boot is more Russian than he!" Nicolai was saying to himself. "The pigs that make German *wuerstchen* are more Russian than he. The wine he drinks is more Russian than that swine!"

But as he looked at what was in the palm of his hand, his breath stopped and his words with it. Then, because he was a very devout man—because in fact he could not remain in the Russia where priests and all the works of the kind God are so abused, so contaminated with curses, so blocked and thwarted and mocked—because of the very religion in his heart, he crossed himself once, twice, and thrice and he made a little bow such as he always made whenever he passed a holy ikon. For in his hand he found two paper bills and each was for a thousand gold marks.

Two thousand gold marks!

He was a thrifty man, and he had in the bank more than eleven hundred gold marks at that moment, the product of eight years of hard work and close saving, since his flight from an afflicted Russia. And now the heavens had opened

149

upon him and showered him with wealth.

The first words that broke from him were the ones of the Easter greeting which all good members of the Greek church exchange on that loveliest of all the days in the year.

Both the greeting and the answer rushed from the lips of Nicolai, as he whispered: "Christ is risen again! . . . He has, indeed!"

Nicolai put out a hand against the wall and supported himself. He looked again at the money in his hand and blessed himself once more.

And he said to his secret soul: "Our Father in Heaven, hallowed by Thy name. Forgive me the evil thoughts that I had against this man. Explain to me, O God, how such a noble soul, such a great heart, such a devout spirit, could speak such bad thoughts in such bad Russian? Oh God, forgive me the word that I meant to speak against him! Forgive me, bless him, be merciful to all sinners, and bring at last into the peace of Thy Heaven me and my noble lord who wishes the Burgundy!"

When he had paused for this moment and completed his devout thoughts, he sighed, and put the money in his pocket. As he walked on, he kept his hand pressed over the place.

Two slips of printed paper, so small, and yet with such meaning.

It was one of those nothings which are everything. For instance, how many words we speak, and ask for bread and butter, and say good morning, and farewell, and give good wishes in which our hearts have not spoken freely; and yet the same words may contain miraculous meaning. As when on the day of days one speaks to a woman and in her face the light breaks suddenly.

It was like that—a miracle—a something that was nothing—a nothing that was Heaven itself!

150

Nicolai went slowly on into the pantry and there the head butler, fierce, tall, stiff as an old wolf, halted him with a glance.

"Well, but what is he? Is he Russian?" asked the butler.

"Is he Russian?" asked Nicolai. "Is the holy God Russian? Is the blue in the sky a Russian blue? Am I Russian? Is the saint I was named for a good Russian?"

"Ah, well," said the butler, "I see that a dog only needs the right stroke of the whip in order to know his master. He was right when he called you a wine thief, then?"

"Brother," said Nicolai, "I never have tasted more than three swallows of wine in my life, and they were at a wedding, and I was sick and vomited afterward; but if my master says that I am a thief of wine, who am I to say no to him? Pray God that we have some Burgundy in the cellar that is fit for his good lips!"

Chapter Seventeen

"WHAT ARE they doing now?" asked Lady Cecil. "What is happening in the von Emsdorf house?"

"That fellow Gloster is pouring red wine down his throat," said Winton Holling Jones. "He's found a part that he likes to play."

"But *that's* not fair," said Cecil. "He's simply imitating Raskoi, and I think he does it wonderfully."

"It's impossible to play such a part," pronounced Winton Jones, "without a natural inclination. This Gloster— you know him quite well, Cecil?"

"Once I intended to marry him," she answered.

"But no longer?" asked Jones.

"Should you ask me that?"

"My dear," said Jones, "I had intended to give you the entire support, the entire confidence and trust of our service, but if you could give yourself away to a wild, headlong fellow like this Gloster, how could we possibly retain faith in you?"

"You know, you ought to praise him," she pointed out, "because he plays his part so perfectly."

"It may be better to say that he's perfectly cast for it,"

answered Jones, sharply. "But to go back a bit—you've recovered from the infatuation?"

She considered this remark for a moment and then replied in a somewhat dreaming voice, "Jules Cailland is . . ." She didn't finish.

"Is that the answer?" asked Jones, looking into her eyes. She shrugged.

At this, Winton Holling Jones began to look closely at her through his big glasses, but he knew enough about women to say no more at the moment.

"What is happening in von Emsdorf's house?" she repeated.

"We're too late," said Jones. "Even for a Jacquelin, we're too late. Whatever is done has to be done tonight, and what can be done in a single night? In the morning, their plans will be completed, the charts of the Line photographed, and the game is lost!"

"And then?" she asked.

He said, slowly: "Germany—Austria—Italy—Russia—France—England—Belgium . . . Then Japan striking in from the East . . . Turkey reaching for the Greek Islands. And we have a war that will make the Great War look like a skirmish. The world didn't know how to kill in those days. Now we're experts. No matter who wins, democracy is dead and we give ourselves into the hands of dictators. Free speech dies. Thought dies with it."

He sighed. "Turn on the radio," he said, "and let us have something to drown our own words; a mental anaesthetic is what I need when I think of the future."

She crossed her room and turned on the radio. "Music?" she asked.

"Yes, music."

She moved the arrow on the dial. It caught on brief tangles of uproar, tore through them, passed on through loud voices, reached a rich German tenor singing a Viennese waltz.

She turned and looked a question at Jones; he nodded and she tuned the radio so that it gave the words clearly but softly.

Even then, he was not quite satisfied with it.

"Louder, please!" said Winton Jones.

She strengthened the music, watching Winton Jones. He did not give a signal until the tenor was shouting into his ears. Then he leaned back in his chair. She sat on the arm of it.

"That's what the world is coming to," said Jones, his voice half drowned by the uproar. "Let's get used to it, or else be ready to die. . . ."

The music cut off, suddenly, in the midst of a note. Then a loud, harsh German voice spoke, clipping off the words with well-trained enunciation.

"The police want Gregor Raskoi. G-r-e-g-o-r R-a-s-k-o-i . . . Russian . . . For murder, the police want Gregor Raskoi for murder . . . He stands six feet tall, and weighs about a hundred and ninety pounds. Blond . . . loud voice . . . a confident step but a light one . . . clean shaven . . . Speaks good German . . . Constantly singing either in German or Russian. He drinks much red wine. The police want the Russian, Gregor Raskoi, for the murder of William Gloster, an American. . . ."

Lady Cecil cried out. Jones caught her by the hand.

"Don't you understand?" he demanded.

"Yes. Now I remember . . ." she answered, faintly.

The police had ended their SOS. The radio orchestra valiantly and with German precision struck back into their song at exactly the point at which the interruption had cut them off. The well trained tenor began on the very note with the violin.

154

Jones looked at the stone-pale face of the girl and said nothing for a moment; she kept waiting, haunting him with her eyes.

"Well?" asked Jones at last. "How long will it take them to locate Gloster and arrest him for killing himself?"

"He's been as easy to see in Berlin as a red flag. He's carried bottles of wine in his hand up and down the street."

"They'll have him before long," said Jones, nodding. "Besides, the radio may be heard in the house of von Emsdorf, by the servants. We must bring word to Gloster."

"I shall," said Lady Cecil.

"You will?" repeated Jones, smiling a little. "How will you break into the house?"

"I don't know," said the girl. "But I do know that I'll manage to reach him."

In the house of von Emsdorf, Count di Parva had straightened in his chair at the dinner table to say, "We have the energy. We have the will. But two great peoples are throttled for lack of breathing space. They are prevented from growing up by the lack of colonial space. Sooner or later they must strike, and they are insanely foolish unless they strike together. The object for attack is equally at hand, as von Emsdorf points out. It is France, with her enormous and unexploited colonial empire. If Italy attacks from the south and Germany from the west, will England intervene? I think not. England is not ready. She has commenced an enormous program of military and naval rehabilitation; she is spending a billion dollars a year to equip herself for the struggle; but she is not ready now. The lesson of the World War she will not quickly forget.

"At that time she flung herself into northern France and sacrificed the men of her regular army to impede the German advance. Then she advanced a huge army which passed through the four years of hell on the western front. In return for these immense sacrifices she now receives not even the most casual gratitude from France. It is taken for granted that she fought only to preserve her own safety. She did not find France a willing ally in the recent Ethiopian affair. And I feel certain that England will remain—no matter how unwillingly in some senses—apart from the battle at least for a time.

"Before long, however, her peace-loving people will see that they cannot endure a German frontier immediately across the channel. Then they will fight. There would be in the hands of Germany and Italy only a few early weeks in which they could work unhampered by the enormous force of England. What could they accomplish in those weeks? I think we all have considered it.

"The Italian forces have a region of huge mountains to penetrate unless they choose to try to work along the Mediterranean coast, where the terrain is very narrow and the fortifications of France are very strong. The Italian advance, at the best, can only occupy a percentage of the French army, and not the majority of it. To the north, there remains the great German attack. Impeded by the lack of great guns and heavy tanks, units of immense cost, the German army may rush over the frontier quickly, but there it finds a terrible obstacle. I refer to the Maginot Line!

"No doubt we all understand something about the Line, but for my part I have spent three months in as close examination as possible, and at the end of that time, I felt that the Line was invincible. It is a series of forts, sometimes connected by underground passages, and sometimes isolated. But the forts are of enormous strength. We have to conquer, in them, bastions of concrete twenty feet thick, which the most powerful bombs cannot break open. In

156

them we meet with vast underground barracks where soldiers may rest from the fighting in places where even the thunder of a bombardment cannot reach their ears. The shock units and the reserves are both housed on the actual fighting line! Therefore fresh men continually will be serving the guns.

"Now imagine what this means to an attacking army which has pushed forward with great enthusiasm, let us say, and is ready to deliver a great massed attack to break through the obstacle.

"While it is still miles away from the Maginot Line, its masses of troops pour down the highways; they stream across the country, they enter the gullies, they pass into the villages, they occupy the ridges, the woods, the paths, the ravines. All of them feel secure because of distance or because of the natural shelter of some sort that screens them from the eyes of the enemy. But now consider what happens.

"From high observation balloons, and from scouting airplanes, messages are rushed back by the French. The position of every body of German troops is given. Words are not needed. Mere numbers will do. The defenders check off the reported numbers on their accurate charts, already prepared. At once the range for every gun, big and small, is known for every target that lies across the front.

"There is no question of missing. The guns are pointed with as much accuracy as though they were shooting at open targets and at pointblank range. The woods are covered with a stream of shells. A high, angling fire drops explosives, shrapnel, and gas over every recess behind the ridges. The villages, many of them already mined, are blown off the face of the earth.

"Suppose, in spite of this hell of fire, the Germans stream forward. Their ranks are decimated. Half the combatants are dead or wounded. But still they thrust ahead. They encounter then a forest of steel beams through which their charging tanks cannot penetrate. They encounter, also, mined ground, and barbed-wire entanglements prepared for years. What can break through on a broad front against such opposition?

"But suppose that miracles happen and the foremost lines are penetrated? Still the forts maintain a terrible fire from their turrets. And other forts set back behind the foremost lines now open with direct fire. Thousands of rapid-fire guns, tens of thousands of machine guns water the earth with lead. What further advance is possible? In twenty-four hours the finest army in the world could be paralyzed and pulverized by a single attack against those invincible defenses. Gentlemen, I come to a pause. I wait for some answer."

Di Parva ended; Johann Gleich made the only comment during the gloomy moment of silence that followed. "Von Emsdorf, can you speak?' he asked.

Von Emsdorf rose and smiled on them. "Consider the strongest man in the world," he said, "and what a fine surgeon could do to him by severing the nerves of a single nerve center? His body would be paralyzed, would it not?"

"It would," said the cold voice of Johann Gleich.

"My dear friends," said von Emsdorf, "our spies, of course, have penetrated the secret of the Maginot Line. They are ready to cut a few of the nerve centers of that Line."

"What are the nerves of the Maginot Line?" asked di Parva.

Gloster burst out, "The electric power lines! Electricity, the brain of the Twentieth Century! Electricity, the soul of the new Russia."

Von Emsdorf stared at Gloster for a moment. "Our

friend Gregor Raskoi is exactly right," he said. "We shall cut the electric lines of a central section of the fortifications; and the whole body of the Maginot Line will be like a body whose spinal column has been severed!"

Louvain remarked, "Those lines must be, most of them, deeply buried, defended in every possible way. Besides, the system must be so intricate that it could be deciphered only on the master charts of the Maginot Line; and God knows those charts are safe in Paris defended by the entire ingenuity and force of the French Republic."

Von Emsdorf was still on his feet. He smiled on Louvain.

"My dear fellow," he said, "you may have been somewhat surprised when I added to our intimate little circle Monsieur Jules Cailland? I may give you one reason for that addition now. The master charts of the Maginot Line no longer are in Paris. What copies they may have, I don't know. But the original of the plans was abstracted from the place of safekeeping in Paris by the extraordinary talent of Monsieur Cailland."

Gloster shouted, "Then, by God, we already are riding down the Champs-Elysées! We are walking through the wine cellars of Burgundy. We are already drunk. We have filled our pockets with the jewels of the Rue de la Paix."

"Is it true?" asked Johann Gleich, turning white with joy.

"It is true," said von Emsdorf. "I will tell you a very brief story. Monsieur Cailland, having taken the plans, despatched them to Germany by a safe messenger. Monsieur Cailland then drew attention from his activity in that direction by beginning the publication of a series of articles about the celebrated Monsieur Jacquelin; all of you have read those articles with amazement and pleasure. But while Jules Cailland was publishing the articles, his messenger was stopped in Germany by the long arm of another power.

Can you guess what power, gentlemen? Not France, I assure you."

"By England," suggested Johann Gleich. "She has the finest secret service in the world."

"By England," nodded von Emsdorf. "Her agents operated with miraculous speed, intercepted the messenger, gained the plans from him, and returned them. Not to Paris —ah, trust the clever English not to have done that immediately—but to London. It was then my painful duty, gentlemen, to fly to London myself. I will not tell you the trail I followed. It is sufficient for you to know that at a certain time tea was served in a room in London to a female English spy who had been instrumental in regaining the plans. She was honored by the presence of a number of important dignitaries. There were so many important men in the room that it was impossible for them to pay any attention to the underlings who carried the tea trays back and forth. Therefore your friend von Emsdorf was able to enter, and when he left the room he was carrying the briefcase which contained the plans."

He could not help throwing back his head with a smile of triumph.

"Oh, little Western peoples," Gloster said, "win your wars with pieces of paper. Get fat eating one another. Mother Russia will swallow you all, one day!"

There was a soft murmur from the others at the table. Johann Gleich, turning brilliant eyes on Cailland, said intensely.

"Monsieur Cailland, you have changed the history of the world!"

Cailland waved the praise away with both hands and a modest laugh.

"I am about to lay everything before you!" said von Emsdorf, and left the room.

Here one of the servants came in and stood behind the chair of Gloster. He tried to keep his voice to a whisper, but his panting excitement made every word clearly audible, as he said: "Herr Raskoi, an SOS has been sent out by the police describing you and asking for your apprehension as the murderer of an American, William Gloster!"

Gloster leaned back in his chair, yawned, and swallowed a glass of the Burgundy.

"They are too far away to matter," he said. "The Americans are much too far away to matter. It will be a long time before Russia notices them, and then swallows them. A good, fat bite. Perhaps the last one that Russia will need to take before she owns the world!"

Johann Gleich said, "Is he drunk?"

"No. He's just Russian," smiled Louvain.

"Do you realize, Raskoi," said Gleich, "that the police will have you in their hands within a few hours?"

"They will have something worthwhile, then," said Gloster. "And God teach them to enjoy me!"

A voice cried out in the library. The sound of it made Gleich leap up from his chair. "That is von Emsdorf!" he exclaimed.

"What would he be yelling about?" asked Gloster. "The police don't want him, do they?"

They heard two or three blows struck. Friedrich der Grosse growled like a devil. Then von Emsdorf reappeared in the doorway that led to the library.

His face was a bright crimson, with white spots painted on the center of each cheek.

"Ah-ha!" cried Gloster in a great voice. "Look at him! Look at him! He couldn't do what he promised. Has he lied to us, then?"

Von Emsdorf said, "Cailland!"

"Ah?" answered the Frenchman.

"Were you with Gregor Raskoi every moment since he entered the house?"

"Either I or the servants," said Cailland.

"He is the only one who could approach Friedrich der Grosse without having his throat torn out," said von Emsdorf. "And the plans of the Maginot Line have been taken from the place where the dog was guarding them. Raskoi— you are the thief!"

Chapter Eighteen

"WAIT HERE," said Holling Jones, when they had come down the alley to the great, dark rear of von Emsdorf's house. "Stay for me here, Cecil. I'll bring the car around near the mouth of the alley and then come back to you."

She stood back against the alley wall, facing the house, and looked up at the lighted windows. There were not many of them. Three or four, only, sent out rectangular patches of light which glowed obscurely on the opposite wall. Even the rear face of the building was imposing, big pilasters springing up to classical capitals above which the heavy cornice rose.

Kitchen noises came out to her obscurely and sometimes a vague sound of laughter—a mere pulse of it rather than a distant voice. A footfall moved discreetly towards her up the alley. It did not come from the direction of Jones. Therefore she turned, drew the collar of her cloak closer about her face, and walked very very slowly down the side of the wall as the footfall approached, was passing her, and then halted. She stopped in turn, for a girl stood beside her in the shadow.

"As?" said the voice of Elise. "Are you thinking of him,

163

also? Do you know?"

"Know what?" asked Lady Cecil, drawing back close to the wall.

The other girl followed and stood near. "The police . . ." she said.

"I know," answered Lady Cecil.

"We have to reach him!" said Elise. "Is that why you are here?"

"Yes. And I don't know how. . . ."

"There'll be a chance of some sort," said Elise. "You care for him?"

"Yes," answered Lady Cecil.

"Then go away and keep yourself for him," said Elise.

"Would you stay here alone?"

"Don't you see?" answered Elise. "What happens to me doesn't matter in the least. I'm only a gesture in the dark. There's no brightness or use left in me. And I owe him something."

"You owe him something?"

"Raskoi is dead!" said the girl. "The beast, Raskoi! Do you know what I saw? I saw that terrible Raskoi driven back by the fists of Gloster. I heard the knuckles smacking against his face. The blood flew out in thin sprays. He could have killed Raskoi with his hands! If I'd only waited, I might have seen him do it. But I was hungry for the end. So I used the bottle and struck at the back of his head."

"It was not he that struck down Raskoi?" asked Lady Cecil.

"Do you think he would strike any man from behind?" said Elise.

Here a thin, vague square of light fell all about them, flashing on a small pool of water that had formed on the pavement. The rear door of von Emsdorf's house had opened.

164

"Don't move! Stand still!" whispered Elise. "If we don't move they may not see us!"

Two men stood in the illuminated doorway. As they stirred, their broad shadows swayed across the eyes of Lady Cecil. She could see past them down a long hall. The voices of the two sounded dimly.

"Go to headquarters, Anton," said one.

"I would rather go to hell," said Anton.

"No one else will believe you, however."

"There is a man often on duty two blocks from here," said Anton. "I know him, and he might believe me."

"But anyway it can't be the right man they have here."

"No? I tell you that I've heard the name used in the dining room. 'Raskoi.' I've heard them call him 'Raskoi.' I'm going to find my friend at the police, now. Where did you say they'd put Raskoi?"

"In the corner room on the third floor. And he's guarded there like a handful of pure gold."

"Come along with me. If my man's at his post, you won't be away for two minutes."

But the other hesitated.

"Suppose that I'm called for in the meantime?"

"It doesn't matter. They won't suspect. Come with me."

"I haven't the key to the door."

"Leave it a little ajar. Hurry!" urged Anton.

The other turned and looked down the brightly lighted hall. Then he stepped out, decisively, and drew the door softly shut behind him. A single long ray still escaped from the edge of it into the night. The two walked off up the alley with sharply clicking heels.

"It means that we're too late!" said Elise.

"I'm going in. There'll be no better chance," said Lady Cecil.

"Going in? You can't go in," whispered Elise.

"Wait here!" answered Lady Cecil. "A short man with a huge head and large glasses—he'll be back in a moment. Tell him that I've gone inside."

"You can't . . ." pleaded Elise.

But Lady Cecil, shaking off that restraining hand, crossed the alley hurriedly. She had to go swiftly for fear her own thoughts would overtake her. And reaching the door she pulled it open and felt a whispering shadow reach vainly at her from behind.

That was Elise, of course. But she stepped on inside and pulled the door shut behind her until, as before, it was only open a crack. It was a barrier that Elise dared not open, it appeared, and Cecil went softly down the hallway.

She thought of pulling off cloak and hat in the hope that her black dress might make her look like a uniformed servant of the house. But she knew from Jones that there were no women in the place. If she were seen there would be no doubt as to why she was in the residence of von Emsdorf. And von Emsdorf himself could not help but know her face. So she went on, softly, steadily, with a vague feeling that if she kept moving her mind would tell her what to do and where to go, and with a certain knowledge that if she paused a sickness of fear would overcome her.

The smell and the moist warmth of new cookery lived in the air of the hallway; and the kitchen noises clinked and rattled to her left.

The corridor turned and at a sharp angle entered a great hall. At the base of the hall a double stairway curved towards the next floor and she hurried for this at once, blessing the thickness of the rug that deadened her footfall.

The chandelier above her showered brilliance into the long mirrors. She saw her image drift through a galaxy of reflected stars, like something that swam deep in illumined water, a dark shadow. Then her foot was on the first step of the right-hand stairway.

That was when she heard the descending footfalls. Whether they took the left or the right hand way down, they were sure to see her in another few seconds. She turned, therefore, and fled down the hall. A great, square portal, columned on either side in varicolored marble, offered her an entrance into another room and she hurried into a big, dim library.

A fire smoldered and smoked on a huge hearth; one floor lamp threw a round pool of light on the pattern of a Persian rug. Otherwise the big room was dark. The leather bindings filled the shelves with a faint shimmering of color, except for the vellums which stood out like birch trees in a moonlit forest.

The voices of two men continued down the hall behind her. One, she thought with a leap of the heart, was the voice of Cailland. But that comforting hope was lost from her mind when something moved in the dimness at the end of the room. Right up from under a desk rose a dog as big as a wolf and watched her with pale green eyes.

She shrank away. The beast stood with its head down, pointing in her direction as though it were about to charge, yet remained fixed in place. Here the voices in the hallway abruptly turned into the entrance of the room. A big couch near a window was the only shelter, though it would shield her from only a part of the room. She dropped down behind it and lay flat with her chin on her folded arms.

She almost forgot her danger, a moment later, when she definitely recognized the voice of Cailland, saying:

"If we put a bit of pressure on him, he may forget his part and lapse back into himself. But I'd advocate a bit of sharper action."

"How far did you get with him?" asked von Emsdorf.

"Farther than he liked," said Cailland.

"What first made you suspect him?" asked von Emsdorf.

"If one starts adding together the little impressions which make a suspicion," said Cailland, "often they hardly total a single unit. But you surely are aware of that."

"Well, naturally. But I'm stricken, Jacquelin."

"If you please!" urged Cailland, softly.

"That name seems to frighten you to death!" snapped von Emsdorf. "It's your own, isn't it?"

"That name," answered Cailland, "will cut my throat some day."

"Isn't the suspicion about your identity spread everywhere now? Since *La Liberté* printed that last article about you and suggested that you were yourself the man you had been writing about. . . ."

"A hundred people will be willing to swear that I am not that famous man."

"Let the name go," said von Emsdorf. "But now tell me more in detail exactly what happened?"

"The police are sending out the SOS about the murder at stated intervals, as you know," said Cailland. "In the last one, they gave a very full description of the dead body which had been found in the apartment of Gregor Raskoi. That was when the first thought came over me."

"Which was what?" asked von Emsdorf. "I heard that same description and nothing struck me particularly in it."

" 'About six feet tall,' " quoted Cailland. " 'Weight about a hundred and ninety pounds. Blond. Age just past thirty . . .' Doesn't that sound familiar to you?"

"In what respect?"

"Why, it describes the dead man in the closet at Raskoi's apartment and it also describes the man in this house who is calling himself Raskoi!" said Cailland.

The girl, behind the couch, gathered herself suddenly. She made in the darkness a screaming face and then pressed both hands over her mouth.

Von Emsdorf was saying, "By God, Cailland, I begin to guess what you mean!"

"I've been talking Russian to him," said Cailland, "and one thing seems reasonably clear. He's not Russian!"

"But Nicolai identified him!" exclaimed von Emsdorf.

"Did you see him shake hands with Nicolai at the table, when they were talking?" asked Cailland.

"Yes. I remember."

"Well, what may he have left in Nicolai's hand?" asked Cailland.

Von Emsdorf snapped his fingers. He had moved with Cailland, now, to a place close by the hearth. The light was sufficiently dim so that the glow of the fire threw their unshapely images against the wall; flickers of the living flame tossed these shadows into gross movement.

If she could see the speakers, of course they could see her. But she forgot her danger as she listened to Cailland.

"The point is," the Frenchman was saying, "that if the man in the house is not a Russian, he is most certainly the American of whose murder Raskoi is accused."

"Bei Gott!" cried von Emsdorf.

"Simple, I'd say. Wouldn't you?" asked Cailland. "You can see how it happened. The American, as everyone knows, is a playboy millionaire who runs around the world hunting for adventure. Well, if he met Raskoi I suppose that the adventure seemed very good, indeed. He makes friends with the Russian. They begin to drink together in Raskoi's rooms. They fight. William Gloster brains Raskoi with the bottle. But in the meantime, he has heard enough about the reasons why Raskoi has come to Germany, from Raskoi himself. He has to disguise himself in order to make his escape from the German law on account of the murder. Isn't that clear?

169

"So he kills two birds with one very pretty stone. He puts on the clothes of Raskoi and assumes his name at the same time. He acts out the usual behavior of that drunken Russian, though of course Louvain did not recognize his face. He could not be sure that this fellow was the real Raskoi he had seen in Russia. Naturally not! In the house with us we have not Raskoi at all, but William Gloster, adventurer-extraordinary. Isn't it all clear?"

"Perfectly clear!" said von Emsdorf. "I think we can hand the fellow over to the police and let them deal with him for us."

"Hand him over to the police, then," said Cailland, ironically. "And guess what Gloster will tell the police about this house and what goes on in it."

"True. Then we must handle him ourselves," said von Emsdorf.

"That is obvious," agreed Cailland.

"And, as a matter of fact, I think that I'll turn the thing over to you."

"Ah, von Emsdorf," said Cailland, "can't you give the dirty work to another pair of hands?"

"I cannot," said von Emsdorf. "I don't know of a man or a friend I have in the house whom I could trust to do this business in the proper way. Once he is dead, you can dispose of his body in the streets, easily. When he is found, the police will be too glad of the finding; they will not be asking how the murderer's body came to be left on the pavement. But ah, *Gott,* Cailland . . . what a frightful gap it leaves in our plans to have Russia unaccounted for at our backs while we go forward against France—if we *can* go forward at all, now that the Maginot plans are lost to us!"

"When I have finished with Monsieur Gloster," said Cailland, cheerfully, "I'll undertake the finding of the plans, my dear friend."

"Jacquelin!" breathed von Emsdorf. "I can't help the name coming to my lips. I know, suddenly, that you will do as you promise."

"Ah," murmured Cailland, "but what's the trouble with our friend Friedrich der Grosse? I thought he was to do penance by being kept there under the desk the entire night?"

"I should skin the worthless cur alive," said von Emsdorf. "But this is as strange as the very devil. Is he stalking something?"

"He may be sleepwalking," chuckled Cailland, "and hunting the ghost of a deer in his sleep!"

"He's certainly hunting," said von Emsdorf, "but there's no sleep in the green of his eyes."

"Look!" said Cailland.

Around the edge of the couch appeared the big head of Friedrich der Grosse, pointing straight towards the girl. She heard von Emsdorf shout out something at the same instant and saw him come running.

There was nothing else to do. She stood up and looked her danger in the eye.

Chapter Nineteen

VON EMSDORF, when he saw her, drew himself up short and then came slowly on.

"Monsieur Cailland," he said, "I present to you an unexpected guest, and an unexpected pleasure. Lady Cecil, this is Jules Cailland. Or have you just heard me mention him under another name?"

She looked from von Emsdorf to Cailland and let her eyes rest on the Frenchman with profound and perfect loathing. Cailland bowed to her and turning his back, walked toward the hearth.

"The truth is," said von Emsdorf, "that she must have heard me call you by another name, Cailland. And what can we do about that?"

Cailland said nothing. He made a French gesture of surrender with both hands. Still he refused to look at the girl.

"Will you tell me, Lady Cecil," said von Emsdorf, "what brought you into my house? It couldn't have been your old interest, could it? It couldn't have been the Maginot plans?"

She said nothing. She could not take her eyes from Cailland.

Then she heard von Emsdorf saying, "There's only one really safe room in the house. Will there be any harm in putting her there, while we make up our minds what to do with her? Lady Cecil, forgive me, but you see that something must be done with you?"

She could not speak.

"And so," said von Emsdorf, with a gesture, "if you come with us upstairs . . . Later on, perhaps you'll be encouraged to tell us why you came, who came with you, how you entered the house, and other details? Cailland, you'll accompany us like a good fellow, won't you?"

Cailland walked behind them up the hall, up the stairs. He did not utter a word.

Von Emsdorf went on, "That dear friend of my country and of me—Mr. Winton Jones—has he sent you? His pride in you, that day in London, was a beautiful thing, dear Lady Cecil. It was more than the pride of a father in a child. It was the pride of an Englishman in an Englishwoman—young—so wise—so lovely . . ."

He could not help laughing a little.

They reached the upper hall; they climbed to the third story. The ceiling was lower, but still there was an air of magnificence about the house. The deep red carpet whispered and crinkled under their feet; and so they came to a door outside of which two men walked up and down.

They drew themselves up and stood back for the master of the house to pass.

"We enter here," said von Emsdorf to them. "For the moment, until you have other instructions, you'll watch this lady as carefully as you watch the gentleman who is already in the room."

He drew the door open.

"Company for you, Herr Gloster!" he called from the doorway, and ushered the girl before him into the room.

173

Gloster stood up from the table at which he sat. He had thrown off his coat on account of the heat of the evening and rolled up his shirt sleeves over the thick of his forearms. He looked like a laborer taking his ease at the end of the day.

"You see, my kind American friend," said von Emsdorf, "that I think constantly of your comfort and I leave the lady here to entertain you and to be entertained. Herr Gloster, must I present you?"

The girl went to Gloster and put her arms around his neck. He patted her shoulder but did not kiss her upturned face.

"So?" said von Emsdorf. He laughed.

"Stay a while, Cailland," he ordered. "I have to think about this from several angles. And then we'll talk it all over."

He left the room. The three of them remained in a silence as the girl turned slowly from Gloster and faced Cailland.

"I heard him, Willie," she said. "I heard the great Jacquelin—the brilliant Frenchman—I heard him talking with von Emsdorf when they couldn't know that I was near them. Willie, he told von Emsdorf who you are—he told him that it was Raskoi who was dead. I heard him, like a traitor and a coward, behind your back—like a coward! like a coward! . . . Willie, I'm sick at heart. Will you look at him? Do you see now what the face of a traitor is like?"

"De Waters," said Gloster, "be yourself and step down a bit from the high horse. I'm already in deep trouble. Cailland tells von Emsdorf almost everything . . . and von Emsdorf makes Cailland take direct charge of me—and of you! My dear De Waters, use your brain. If we have a ghost of a chance to get away from this devil of a von Emsdorf, Cailland has secured the chance for us now. Could anything be clearer than that?"

Cailland lifted his head, which had fallen slightly as he stared at the two of them.

"As a matter of fact," said Gloster, "it's one of those characteristic Jacquelin strokes, isn't it? He seems to give away everything, and that is just the moment when he is about to get everything."

"Jules!" said the girl. "Is it true?"

He shrugged his shoulders, answering, "Talk over the truth of it with Gloster, Cecil."

"It *is* true!" she murmured. "And I've been a gross fool! Jules, will you forgive me?"

"My dear Cecil," said the Frenchman, "of course I forgive you."

"De Waters, step over there to the window and admire the view. Cailland, come into this corner and let's talk."

He went with Cailland into the farthest corner of the room, and said softly:

"You'd sold us to von Emsdorf, had you?"

"I did not say——" began Cailland.

"You don't need to say," answered Gloster. "The fact's as clear as the nose on my ugly face. I saw the crook in your look when you came into the room. But whether as Jacquelin or Cailland, will you talk sense and good business with me, old fellow?"

"Well?" asked Cailland, staring at the American.

"Without you," said Gloster, "we're lost. She's lost. I'm lost. And the Maginot plans will go back into German hands. Which means fifty kinds of hell for the rest of the world. But if you're true to us, we may have all our chances back."

Cailland shook his head slowly.

"You're back on the same footing you were on before, with her," said Gloster. "Does von Emsdorf offer a greater chance than that to you?"

"Nothing in the world means so much," whispered Cailland.

"We both want her, Jules. If you let von Emsdorf wipe me out, you'll never have her. If you join the Germans, you'll never have her. But if you fight it out on our side, you have more than an even chance. Nothing in the world can keep her from you. You'll be the great Jacquelin again, in her mind. Who can stand against you then?"

Cailland turned his head, gradually, as though an invisible hand were forcing his chin around. He stared at the girl for a second or so before he glanced back.

"There are things you know about me," he said, whispering the words.

"I forget them," said Gloster, instantly.

"Do you mean that you give her up?" asked Cailland.

"No, by God!" murmured Gloster. "But if we come away with the Maginot plans, I forget everything except that without you we never could have succeeded."

Cailland began to snap his fingers softly, as though he were counting money. After a while, he said, "I'm going through the house to see how many people are up. That fellow Gleich is a cat who never sleeps. Von Emsdorf will probably be stirring, also. And I have to get rid of the two men outside this door." He left the room.

"It's all right," said Gloster. "He's going to try to help us out of this muddle. Turn around and talk to me, De Waters, will you?"

"I'm sick," she said. "Sick at heart."

"Being frightened is almost the same as being sad," said Gloster. "You're frightened, Cecil."

"Maybe—partly," she said.

"Turn around and talk to me," said Gloster.

But she shook her head, slowly, and did not turn.

176

"I don't want to look at you, Willie," she answered.

"Are you going to weep, or something?" he asked.

"Willie!" she exclaimed in a breaking voice.

"I'm not going to be nice to you," said Gloster, "if that's what you mean."

She caught a sobbing breath.

"I'll tell you what's the matter with you," said Gloster.

"I don't want to know," she said, shaking her head.

"It's something that time will take care of, De Waters."

"Don't use that name!"

"You're young, De Waters, and time will take care of that. Quite a lot of time."

"Willie, you want me to cry. You're trying to make me cry," said the girl.

"Being young," said Gloster, "you're naturally fickle. Some youngsters are not fickle but that's because they've had a good bringing up. The countess never put a hell of a lot of time on your bringing up, did she? And as for the earl—"

"Stop it!" commanded the girl, whirling about at him.

"As for the earl," said Gloster, "he had to think about those polo ponies, and how could he spare time to think about De Waters, I ask you?"

"You are vulgar, and cheap, and American, and awful, and—Willie, please love me a little!" said the girl.

"Not a damned bit," said Gloster, lighting a cigarette. "Look at all the time, brain power, and hard cash I invested in loving you in those old days, De Waters. All wasted. All brushed out the moment the great cutthroat, spy and liar, Jacquelin, appears on the scene."

"How easy it would be to despise you, Willie!"

"And even Jacquelin, at the first touch of suspicion, goes down the laundry chute along with the other soiled ideas of yesteryear."

177

"I thought he had betrayed you!"

"Darling, if you ever fall in love with a man I'll tell you how to know the real thing. Treachery and lying and cheating and all that sort of stuff won't really matter. You'll love him anyway. The wrong things he does won't be a slap in your face; they'll be a stroke on your heart—what sort of a heart have you, De Waters, anyway?"

"Ah, now I see," she murmured.

"You see what?"

"You didn't want me all wet and soggy with tears; so you've been slapping my face to rouse me a little."

"Don't be so vain, De Waters," he told her. "I'm simply telling you a few selected truths."

She shook her head. "There's always some kindness behind whatever you do."

"I'm a sort of a universal uncle. Is that it?" he asked.

"Willie, do you know what was breaking me down, just now? It was realizing that my fault is what has brought you into horrible danger, here. If I hadn't had my eyes closed with sickening vanity, that day in London, the plans never would have been lost."

"Stop worrying about me," he advised. "Worry a little about yourself. To a von Emsdorf, human beings are units; that's all. Male or female doesn't make a great deal of difference. If he thinks that it's dangerous to have you alive, he'll have you dead. Put that in your pipe and smoke it a while. About the plans"—he snapped his fingers—"I don't care a rap about that. It happened. That's all."

She walked up and down the floor a moment and he watched her from head to foot until she stopped, very close to him.

"Willie, there may not be very much time. We know that."

"That's fairly apparent," said Gloster.

"If you'll hold me a moment and tell me you love me, I think I can tell you that my whole heart is yours forever and ever—if you're really interested, Willie."

"And suppose Jules Cailland begins to be brilliant and dazzling?" said Gloster.

"I'm not going to suppose. I want you, Willie."

"You're not going to have me," said Gloster. "We're going to wait till we're all dead or all out of this pickle. Then we'll see what De Waters has in her funny little English heart."

"Willie, suppose we die and I've never—"

The door opened on Cailland. "There's no one about," he said. "Even Gleich is in his room. I heard him pacing up and down, but at least he's not prowling through the house like a midnight cat. I've sent the two guards from this door to the front of the house. We'll try to get out into the back alley. . . ."

"Winton Jones is somewhere out there with a fast car," said Lady Cecil.

"It's going to be simple, after all," said Cailland, and passed a big service automatic to Gloster.

"Because you make it simple, Cailland," said Gloster.

Chapter Twenty

Gloster went first, feathering his toes so that he glided silently down the hall, and down the windings of the great stairway. When he had reached the main hall on the first floor, he looked back and saw the girl beside Cailland, descending slowly.

Then the voice of Johann Gleich said from above:

"Well, Monsieur Cailland? Well?"

"Ah—Gleich!" called Cailland, turning, making his voice cheerful.

"You have the lady with you," said Gleich. "But where is the man?"

"Safe in the room, back there," said Cailland.

"You lie!" shouted Gleich. "The room is empty, and you're sneaking away with the pair of them. Cailland, put up your damned hands or I'll shoot. You French fox— you fat-faced rat . . . Von Emsdorf! Louvain! Do you hear?"

Gloster, standing back by the entrance to the library, ran suddenly back into the big room and kneeled by a lower shelf. His hands instantly found the stiff, thick folds of paper and he rose with them tucked under his left arm.

180

The shouting of Gleich kept ringing through the house. The front door of the building slammed as Gloster ran back to the library entrance. Then he heard the voice of von Emsdorf crying out:

"Coming, Gleich! Coming! What is wrong?"

"Sneaking, damned treachery!" shouted Gleich.

Cailland had not moved from his place on the stairs. He stood there with his hands above his head, and the girl close to him, their heads bent back to stare up at the approaching figure of Gleich, who came down with a cautious, gliding pace from step to step, holding his gun leveled with the greatest care, and a look of pale concentration in his strange face. Footfalls began to beat down the higher stairs.

"Gleich—I'm sorry!" called Gloster.

He waited a tenth part of a second until the eyes and the gun of Gleich had found him. Then he fired. Johann Gleich made a long blind step into the air and pitched rolling down the stairs. The girl and Cailland ran after that lunging body. They reached the lower hall and turned at full speed into the back hall, with Gloster behind them. The body of Gleich had struck the hall floor and skidded; the gun was still gripped in his hand.

There was only a vague light in the rear hall, but enough to show Cailland lurching to the side, striking the wall, spinning, and the running on again, staggering. He kept one hand pressed to his body. The girl took the other arm over her shoulders, and with the roar of the gunshot from behind in his ears, Gloster turned and saw Gleich leaning on one hand with his automatic, leveling for another shot. Gloster caught him in the sights for a snap shot and fired. The Austrian flattened on his face.

Cailland and the girl had reached the rear door when a figure as big-shouldered as a moose and as long as a moose in the legs ran out from a doorway at Gloster. That was von Emsdorf, who must have taken a rear stairway to come in behind the excitement. He had a gun in each hand and when he saw Gloster he put on the brakes, heaving his body back to stop his impetus. So, slanting back in that manner, he fired point-blank—and missed. Gloster reached in with his own gun and struck the German across the forehead.

A gust of sudden wind struck him. He saw the rear door opening, and the huge body of Cailland tottering out into the night, supported by the girl.

And behind him, down the hall, there were beating footfalls and shouting voices that bellowed in the ears of Gloster like ocean noises in a cave. He ran low, leaning far forward like a young sprinter, and so reached the rear doorway. He snatched the key from the lock, flung the door shut behind him, and locked it from the outside. He was still seeing only one thing—the long arms of von Emsdorf reaching out and fumbling at the air as he fell forward.

Then a bullet clicked through the thick wood of the door. Another crashed on the metal of the lock.

The girl and Cailland still were appallingly close.

As Gloster started for them, two other figures joined them, another woman and a small man.

They helped Cailland forward at a dragging pace, and his head was falling over on one shoulder, and jogging lifelessly up and down with the effort of walking.

Gloster put the loose, dragging weight of that big body over his shoulder and began to run.

He felt the head of Cailland flopping up and down behind him. He heard Cailland groaning: "Let me down. . . . Let me down. . . ."

But Gloster kept on.

Little Winton Jones ran ahead of them and held open the door of a closed car that stood at the corner of the alley. Far behind them, shouting voices broke out into the night air as Gloster, gasping, poured and thrust and hauled the body of Cailland into the machine.

And they were gone, then, swiftly up the street.

The shouting behind them had ended.

Lady Cecil, in the farther corner of the back seat, supported most of the weight of Cailland, as he spilled back against the side of the car, groaning with every breath.

Gloster sat on the other side of him, working at the huge, loose body with rapid hands. Winton Jones drove without too great speed, taking many corners; and Elise was beside him in the front seat, always with her face turned to watch what happened behind her.

Slashing strokes of light from the street lamps cut into the interior of the car, even though the rear curtains were down; and by those glimpses Gloster saw, as he opened the clothes of Cailland, where the bullet had struck. Through the lungs. It must have gone through them. A bubbling sound came in Cailland's breathing, and then Gloster was sure. He took the great bulk into his arms, from the girl.

"We can get a doctor. We've got to stop for a doctor!" she said.

"Not if he were an archangel, my dear," said the calm, small voice of Winton Jones. "We have something with us that's worth more than the life of any man on earth, just now. And we don't stop."

"Willie, make him stop!" cried the girl.

"It's no use," said Gloster.

Cailland stopped the deep, slow groaning.

"D'you mean it?" he asked. "D'you mean . . ." He began to groan again.

Gloster could hear Lady Cecil sobbing, and trying to swallow the sounds. He shook his head when she glanced at him.

Elise, from the front seat, said nothing at all. Her eyes never stopped shifting from Lady Cecil to the wounded man and then, for longer spaces, to the homely face of Gloster.

So the blocks whisked past, hushed moments that were interspersed through the steady, muttering echo of the exhaust, thrown back from the walls on either side. They left the city. They entered the wide hush of the country. And the mind of Cailland had wandered into a far country.

"Give her three points north," said Cailland, "and set that spinnaker, you Lascar rat . . . Spinning Jenny, 1765. . . ."

"He's dying!" murmured Lady Cecil.

"He's dying," agreed Gloster. "Jones, pull up into that lane."

"I'm not stopping," said Jones. "It's still an hour to the airplane."

"Pull up into that lane," commanded Gloster.

Winton Jones pulled the car up into the lane and stopped. The east was turning green with the first of the day, as Gloster dragged the weight of Cailland out of the car and stretched him on the green of a meadow. The night mist was beginning to silver, and two grazing cows looked as big as elephants through the dimness.

Lady Cecil sat down and took the head of Cailland in her lap. He looked very bad—knotted around the eyes as though he were reading fine print, and all the lower part of his face loose as though he were helplessly drunk. The front of his clothes was soggy with his blood. The smell of it was in the air about him.

Winton Jones walked up and down with his hands in his coat pocket; Elise sat on the running-board of the car, mildly indifferent to everything before her.

Lady Cecil kept one hand over the heart of the dying man. "It's almost finished!" she whispered to Gloster. Tears began to run down her face.

"You love him, don't you?" said Gloster.

"He can't be dying!" whispered the girl. "This can't be the end of Monsieur Jacquelin!"

Cailland cried out quite sharply and distinctly, "Jacquelin! Jacquelin!"

Gloster turned his back and lighted another cigarette. Only little Winton Jones tried lamely to comfort her.

Jones said, "Lady Cecil, too many people, suddenly, had come to know him, beginning with von Emsdorf. He had to die. If not today, then tomorrow!"

"But think what's happening," mourned Lady Cecil. "Jacquelin! The great Jacquelin. . . ."

"Jacquelin!" cried Cailland.

Gloster stopped in front of Elise.

"It's going to be a cold ride in the plane with no more clothes than we have," he said.

"Jacquelin!" called Cailland. "The damned horse is dying under me. What shall I do? The horse is failing and they're gaining on us. . . . Jacquelin! I can feel their knives in me, Jacquelin!"

Gloster ran suddenly to Cailland and crouched by him. He took the Frenchman's hands in his. "Jules—d'you hear?" he called.

"Ah. Ah . . ." murmured Cailland. "I thought you had forgotten me, Jacquelin. . . ."

Winton Jones whispered, and somehow they all could hear. "By the living God—it is he!"

Lady Cecil, with both hands lifted to her face, stared at the dying man and his comforter.

"I thought it was happening again," said Cailland, sighing. "I thought I could see the ends of their turbans flapping as they came up on us, Jacquelin. Forgive me. . . ."

"I forgive you," said Gloster. "I am holding your hand, Jules."

"You might have died that day," whispered Cailland.

185

"You took the beaten horse. And I let you take it. . . . Jacquelin, I have been a traitor. . . ."

"Jules, you are my friend," said Gloster. "Do you hear me? Friends—the old days have come back to us. We are one man again!"

"Jacquelin . . ."

"Yes?"

"Do you remember Cairo? And the day you came into the dining room of Shepheard's Hotel with the girl, and you all in a sheik's white robes? My God, how my heart laughed when I saw you! I thought the desert . . . Jacquelin!"

"Yes," said Gloster. "Yes, Jules, I remember your face and the bandage still around your head."

"Jacquelin. I thought the desert had swallowed you. . . . That day I loved you. . . . That day I was worthy. . . ."

He began to cough, and as he coughed, he kicked out his feet violently with the pain. Great red bubbles formed and burst into spray on his lips.

Gloster took him in his arms. Cailland's head fell back. He panted, whispering, "But I was afraid—I was always afraid of the things you made me do, Jacquelin. And at last fear ate out my heart. . . . Jacquelin, I can't breathe. Open the window. . . ."

After a moment, Jacquelin stood up beside the dead man. The others had drawn back toward the car.

"We must go! We must start now!" said Winton Holling Jones. "But ah, what a fool I've been. You tell him, Lady Cecil. I don't want to be the one who breaks in on him, now. Tell him we must start."

"Hush," said the girl. "Are you trying to give orders . . . to Jacquelin?"

186

The phantom spy: a novel of adventu
F BRA   202653

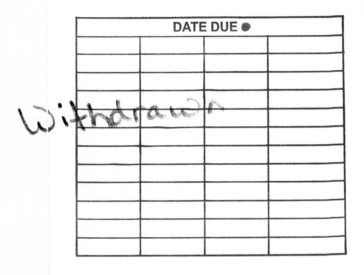

DATE DUE

Withdrawn